# HEALING GRACE

*Practical Steps to Producing Good Fruit
by Replacing Lies with Truth*

EMILY A. EDWARDS, PH.D.
*with*
VALERIE NYSTROM PAINE
LIVING HOPE PUBLISHING
*Midland, TX*

© 2024 Emily A. Edwards, Ph.D. and Valerie Nystrom Paine

All rights reserved. No part of this book may be reproduced in any form or by any electronic or mechanical means, including information storage and retrieval systems, without permission in writing from the publisher except by a reviewer, who may quote brief passages in a review.

Living Hope Publishing
*www.LivingHopePublishing.com*
Design by Valsy Designs

Unless otherwise noted, all Scripture quotations are taken from the New King James Version®. Copyright © 1982 by Thomas Nelson, Inc. Used by permission. All rights reserved.

Scripture quotations marked NLT are taken from the Holy Bible, New Living Translation, copyright © 1996, 2004, 2007, 2013 by Tyndale House Foundation. Used by permission of Tyndale House Publishers, Inc., Carol Stream, Illinois 60188. All rights reserved.

Scripture taken from the New American Standard Bible are marked (NASB). Copyright © The Lockman Foundation 1960, 1962, 1963, 1968, 1971, 1972, 1973, 1975, 1977, 1995. Used by permission. (www.Lockman.org)

Some concepts adapted from materials published by Victorious Christian Living International, 14900 W. Van Buren Street, Building G, Goodyear, AZ 85338. Seven Areas of Life Training® (SALT) Copyright © 2006 by VCLi, Version 2.0 Used by permission. All rights reserved.

ISBN: 979-8-218-48907-6

# CONTENTS

Endorsements .................................................................... vii

Acknowledgments ............................................................... ix

Introduction ....................................................................... xi

Chapter 1 The Fruit Stand Fiasco ........................................ 1

Chapter 2 The Belief Tree .................................................... 7

Chapter 3 Meeting Maximus ............................................. 13

Chapter 4 The Boardroom ................................................ 21

Chapter 5 The Boardroom Follow-Up .............................. 45

Chapter 6 The Prescription ............................................... 51

Chapter 7 Grace-Filled Miracles ....................................... 55

Conclusion ....................................................................... 61

21-Day Challenge For Change .......................................... 63

    Days 1 – 5 Making Good Decisions ............................. 65

    Days 6 – 11 Producing Good Fruit ............................... 79

    Days 12 – 16 5 Truths About God ............................... 97

    Days 17–21 Devotional Prayers .................................. 113

Grace Your Table ............................................................ 125

About The Authors ......................................................... 129

# ENDORSEMENTS

Prepare to connect deeply with the characters in the pages of this book. Their narratives are woven from the fabric of everyday life, mirroring the struggles and triumphs we all encounter. If you've ever grappled with the bad fruit in your life—be it negative thoughts, fractured relationships, or misguided behavior—this book speaks directly to you. Rather than merely pruning the fruit, this book encourages you to delve into the root of the issue.

Embark on an incredible journey of self-discovery as you invite God to unveil the lies you may have unknowingly clung to for years or even decades. These lies manifest as the undesirable fruit in our lives. *Healing Grace* guides you through the process of uprooting these lies and replacing them with the transformative truth of God.

*Healing Grace* is not just a book. It's a roadmap for personal growth and spiritual renewal. With foundations drawn from the Seven Areas of Life Training® series, as seen in *Grace Letters* and *Table Grace*, this book encapsulates principles and diagrams that have consistently proven to catalyze positive change. As Chancellor of *Victorious Christian Life Institute*, where individuals earn their degrees in Biblical Counseling, I can attest that this book accurately portrays how biblical counselors can bring soul-healing and life-change to those they counsel. Emily and Valerie, as exceptional Biblical Counselors yourselves, thank you for gifting us these invaluable tools for profound transformation.

—Dr. Sheryl Nobley
Victorious Christian Life Institute Chancellor

Have you ever had a good friend come alongside you in troubling times, take your hand, and walk with you? Did you feel the comfort that comes from knowing you're not alone, and that someone cares enough to share God's truth with you? As you read *Healing Grace*, you will experience the peace and loving embrace of your Heavenly Father, who loves you and never leaves you.

The beautifully woven story of Grace, both as a person and a teacher, allows God to reveal how He is working through your struggles and experiences, with the intention of turning them for your good. The challenges you are currently facing can be used by God to help others heal.

God's desire, and the purpose of this book, is to empower you to make decisions led by the Spirit and aligned with God's desires, instead of reacting out of flesh and emotions. One path leads to life, the other to death.

It's often said that it takes 21 days to form a new habit, and the 21-Day Challenge for Change is the perfect guide to help you get started. Share this book with a friend and take the challenge together! You'll find it helps you both increase awareness of your daily decisions, draw closer to God, and improve the relationships around you.

I pray that you will realize life is not happening to you, but for you—offering an opportunity to know the TRUTH about God and how He feels about YOU! *Healing Grace* is sure to bear good fruit in the lives of all who read it.

—Marci Nettles
*Broken to Belonging Ministry*
Business Owner | Podcaster | Victorious Christian Life Institute, Class of 2025

# ACKNOWLEDGMENTS

*Emily A. Edwards, Ph.D.*

I would like to thank my husband, Michael. His love and support have been a healing balm for my heart. I am grateful for my wonderful mom and stepdad, Frances and Charlie, my family, my friends, and my church family.

I would specifically like to thank the VCLi staff for allowing us to use these diagrams and principles to share this message.

Most of all, thank You, Heavenly Father, for Your love and acceptance and for the message You gave us to share in this book.

*Valerie Nystrom Paine*

I dedicate this book to my late father, Curtis A. Nystrom, a Christian medical doctor and a messenger of healing grace. When Dad became a Christian at age 45, he told the Lord he would share Jesus with every person who came into his office. He kept that promise and witnessed hundreds saved and healed—spirit, soul, and body.

I am thankful for my loving husband, Fred. He is a constant encouragement to me.

I am grateful for my brother, Rocky Nystrom. I loved the many hours we spent working together on the life-changing discipleship series Seven Areas of Life Training®.

I thank *Victorious Christian Living International* for allowing us to share the concepts contained in this book. They are soul-healing, faith-building, and truth-revealing!

# INTRODUCTION

*Let your roots grow down into Him, and let your lives be built on Him. Then your faith will grow strong in the truth you were taught, and you will overflow with thankfulness. Colossians 2:7 (NLT)*

Have you been frustrated by the bad fruit in your life? Most Christians are. They try to remove it, but then it grows right back. Attempts at plucking fear, sexual immorality, people-pleasing, unhealthy relationships, eating disorders, laziness, and complaining from their lives have been unsuccessful. They harvest bumper crops of negative consequences instead!

If we compare your life to a tree, the fruit represents your good and bad actions, attitudes, emotions, and relationships. Simply picking off the bad fruit doesn't stop the tree from producing more.

In *Healing Grace: Practical Steps to Producing Good Fruit by Replacing Lies with Truth*, Valerie and I share the way to produce more good fruit and less bad fruit. Even while co-writing this book, I was forced to confront my own reoccurring issue. The bad fruit I was seeing was developing relationships with men who saw me as their personal ATM machine or verbal punching bag. However, when I allowed God to start the healing process in me by applying the truths throughout this book, I made different decisions. Today, I'm married to a wonderful, godly man. Maybe like you, I didn't realize I was making poor decisions and believing lies, but my fruit told a different story.

This book, while told as fiction, clarifies that to remove bad fruit, we need to deal with the roots. At the end, you will find a 21-Day Challenge for Change. By taking the challenge, God will reveal the lie and you will be able to remove the lie, replace the lie with truth, and renew your mind. Soon you will be bearing a bumper crop of good fruit!

—*Dr. Emily Edwards*

## Chapter 1

# THE FRUIT STAND FIASCO

*The human heart is the most deceitful of all things, and desperately wicked. Who really knows how bad it is? But I, the LORD, search all hearts and examine secret motives. Jeremiah 17:9–10 (NLT)*

"What a perfect day," exclaimed Grace as she threw her arms heavenward and flopped into the folding canvas chair behind her roadside fruit stand.

It wasn't long before customers arrived, eager to load up on Grace's fresh apples, pears, and plums. Her colorful baskets and trays were piled high and attractively arranged. She grinned and chatted merrily with everyone as she bagged their produce.

Friends and neighbors waited in line to pick out their favorites. Suddenly a dusty, old, red Chevy truck barreled into the parking lot, scattering gravel and dirt over the fruit stand and its patrons. Customers coughed and turned to witness a tall, good-looking man in jeans emerge from the dust cloud like a character in a movie. As the spellbound crowd parted, he tipped his dark cowboy hat. His entrance, as if walking down the perfect Texas-style red carpet, was captured by Grace's customers recording videos with their phones. He paused for several selfies with the crowd, grinned, and then sauntered his way to the front of the line. To get Grace's attention, he pounded out "shave-and-a-haircut-two-

bits" on the fruit stand counter, then winked when she looked up and blushed.

*I knew he liked me when he told me to treat him to dinner. How funny. He's a keeper*, fantasized Grace.

Feeling giddy and shaking with excitement, Grace missed the bag she was filling and dropped several juicy plums on the ground. Grace apologized and decided to throw in a beautiful shiny apple for her customer, but when she reached into her display basket to snag the perfect one, her fingers squished into a rotten blob hidden at the bottom. Grace attempted to remove the spoiled fruit without drawing attention, but as she withdrew her hand, rotten bits of decaying apple dripped from her fingers. Several of her customers made faces and covered their noses. Others hurried to their cars and raced off, including the handsome cowboy. She thought she saw him gesture "loser" with an "L" on his forehead, but she wasn't sure.

Discovering bad fruit at her stand was devastating. *You are a loser*, a chilling voice accused.

Grace shook her head to dispel the dark cloud that had settled over her mind and began studying the brown spots on the apple. With one hand holding her nose, she reached for a stack of disinfectant wipes and demanded in a nasal tone, "Where did you come from, you rotten little stinker?"

Suddenly the scene changed as it does so often in a dream, and Grace found herself beside her beautiful fruit tree, which was now covered with the delightful, red apples everyone sought.

*I love that my fruit blesses so many people.* She smiled as she brushed her hand tenderly over the leaves, but suddenly the memory of her fruit-stand disaster interrupted her thoughts. Happiness vanished as feelings of shame and embarrassment washed over her. First, she remembered her customers' reaction to her rotten fruit, then her dreamy guy-crush mocking her.

## THE FRUIT STAND FIASCO

She muttered, "Well done, Grace! You disappointed a lot of people today with your rotten fruit. Plus, every time a guy comes into your life, you do something ridiculous that spoils what could have been! I don't think there's a man on God's green earth who will ever love and accept you."

Just then, her nose twitched. *What's that smell?* She pulled back a branch on her perfect tree, exposing several little nasties hanging there. "What!" she gasped. "Where did you come from?"

Grace pulled a tissue from her navy-blue work apron to remove the culprits. She discarded the spoiled apples in a nearby trash bin and then inspected the limb. Shock and disbelief washed over her as she watched a handful of small, white blossoms appear on the branch she had just cleared. The dainty petals quickly blew away, and there hung more rotten apples!

Grace grabbed the offending branch, determined to get rid of it. She twisted it from side to side and then up and down. Through clenched teeth, Grace fumed, "Why are you producing rotten fruit?" *Crack!* The branch snapped off the trunk.

Grace dropped to one knee to catch her breath. She rubbed her scraped palms gently before checking the place on the trunk where the branch had been. In those few seconds, the limb had grown back and was loaded with even more spoiled apples.

Grace jumped to her feet in disbelief. She spun around and shouted, "Lord, what is going on? Bad fruit keeps growing back, even when I cut off the branch. I want to get to the root of this!"

As if responding to her call, dark, gnarly roots emerged from the ground and encircled her ankles. As the fibrous fingers tightened, Grace lost her balance and tumbled face down in the dirt with a loud thud. She lay trembling as God began to connect life's dots for her.

*You've been good to me, Lord. My Freedom Wall is filled with the photos of people You have used me to help. Thank You! That's good fruit, but You are showing me there's an unhealthy area in my life that is producing bad fruit.*

Grace rested her chin on her hands for a moment and then said with a sigh, "I have a pattern of unhealthy relationships with men, bad fruit. I know good fruit comes from believing truth and bad fruit is the result of believing lies. Do I believe a lie? If I do, please show me what it is."

Immediately her mind went to the time when she heard her mother talking on the phone. The conversation was as vivid to Grace now as it was that night twenty-five years ago. "Jake, don't you miss the kids? They miss you," her mom said. Then there was a pause. "Oh . . . so you just don't want anything to do with little Grace?"

Grace put her hands over her face and began to sob. "You're right, Lord. The minute I heard that, I believed I was utterly worthless. If my father wouldn't or couldn't love me, how was I going to get another man to love me?"

She thought about how that lie had snaked its way in and through her life. She'd tried to buy men's approval only to be taken advantage of, and her cry for love put her in relationships marked by verbal abuse.

Grace grasped the significance of what the Lord revealed. It was a stumbling block that had tripped her up for years. She prayed with heartfelt gratitude, "Thank You for revealing this lie, Lord. I reject the lie 'I'm not worthy of being loved and accepted.' I choose not to believe it anymore. Remove it from my life. I forgive my father for not wanting anything to do with me. I ask Your forgiveness for the wrong decisions I've made as a result of believing this lie. Please fill the spot where that lie has been with Your truth."

After a few minutes, Grace spoke again, "Lord, what's the truth I need to replace this lie?" She heard a soft scraping sound. She popped up her head and looked around. The first thing she noticed was that her feet were now free from the attack roots. She stood and brushed off her apron and then looked at the trunk of the tree beside her. Grace reached out and traced the newly carved heart and the etched words "Jesus loves Grace."

# THE FRUIT STAND FIASCO

*You want me to renew my mind with that truth, Jesus. Thank You for truly loving and accepting me.*

## Chapter 2

# THE BELIEF TREE

*Blessed is the man who trusts in the LORD, and whose hope is the LORD. For he shall be like a tree planted by the waters, which spreads out its roots by the river, and will not fear when heat comes; but its leaf will be green and will not be anxious in the year of drought, nor will cease from yielding fruit. Jeremiah 17:7–8*

Grace's hammock rocked back and forth as she feverishly copied down the scenes from her dream. *Lord, help me remember everything You revealed! You said the Holy Spirit will teach me all things and bring to my remembrance all things that You said to me.* Grace squeezed her eyes shut to concentrate before the memories drifted away. With a burst of inspiration, she began writing again.

*You described my life as a tree, a tree that bears fruit.*

Beside her notes, she started to doodle. Gradually, she sketched out a tree covered with both good and bad fruit. The good fruit was represented by circles and the bad fruit was represented by ovals. *Shriveled little nasties!*

Fruit
Actions, Emotions,
Attitudes, Relationships

Grace surveyed her masterpiece and pondered its significance. *Lord, You showed me that the fruit represents my actions, emotions, attitudes, and relationships.*

Grace hurriedly jotted down the bad fruit she had experienced: her fear of rejection, spending to buy approval, and the abusive relationships she'd had with men. She then listed the Holy Spirit's good fruit in her life—being a patient listener, a good friend, a compassionate counselor, and a joyful person.

She stopped writing and pondered how, like her, most Christians are bothered when there is bad fruit in their lives. They try to remove it, but in most cases, it just grows back. In her dream, God had shown Grace this fact vividly.

Looking up, she caught the gaze of the faded garden gnome in the neighbor's yard. "The reason it grows back is because the fruit doesn't grow on its own," she explained to the gnome, who appeared to be listening with great interest. "The fruit grows on branches. If our lives were trees, the branches would represent the choices or decisions we make. When we make good decisions, we bear good fruit. When we make bad decisions, we bear bad fruit."

Fruit
Actions, Emotions, Attitudes, Relationships

Branches
Choices, Decisions

She added to her drawing and continued. "Decisions don't just come out of nowhere," she continued. "Just like branches don't just hang by themselves in the air. They are attached to the trunk. If you want to make good decisions, your branches have to be attached to the right kind of trunk. The trunk represents what you value, want, or need in life. So what you value, want, or need (the trunk) drives the decisions that you make (branches), which determines what kind of fruit you will bear (good, bad)." Grace looked down to add to her sketch.

**Fruit**
Actions, Emotions, Attitudes, Relationships

**Branches**
Choices, Decisions

**Trunk**
Values, Wants, Needs

She nodded as she processed the insights God was showing her. *I needed love (the trunk). I wanted my father's love and didn't get it, so I looked to men to fill that need (the branches). That led to a lot of bad relationships and pain (bad fruit).*

Educating the neighbor's gnome continued. "Everyone wants to be loved, accepted, significant, and safe," Grace said, tapping her pen on the paper. "God wants to provide what we need, but if we don't believe He can or will, we'll attempt to meet those needs ourselves or look to other people—like I did."

Holding up her diagram for the gnome to see, Grace recapped, "Here's what we have so far. We all need love." She tapped the trunk of the tree with her pen. "When you look to other people or yourself to fill the need for love, acceptance, or significance, it leads to making bad

HEALING GRACE: Practical Steps to Producing Good Fruit by Replacing Lies with Truth

decisions." Next, she tapped on the branches. "That produces bad fruit." She circled the smaller, more shriveled ovals in her drawing.

Grace was reminded of a verse in James. Resting her writing pad on her lap, she grabbed her phone and quickly looked up the verse and wrote it on her paper: "Yet you don't have what you want because you don't ask God for it." James 4:2 (NLT)

Hmmm. . . . We get upset with God when things go wrong in our lives, but if we're not asking for His wisdom or help, then who's fault is that?

Looking back down, she moved on with her tree illustration, "The trunk of your tree is what you value, but what feeds the trunk?" Hearing no audible reply from the gnome, she answered for him. "The roots," she said. Turning back to her drawing, Grace added a few dark lines to the bottom of her tree trunk to represent the roots.

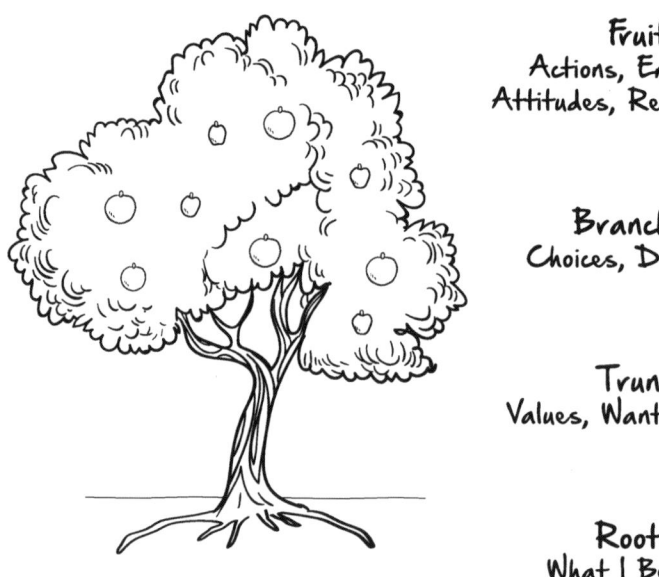

Fruit
Actions, Emotions, Attitudes, Relationships

Branches
Choices, Decisions

Trunk
Values, Wants, Needs

Roots
What I Believe

Still processing the next part of the lesson herself, Grace murmured, "The roots absorb whatever is under the surface and represent what

THE BELIEF TREE

we believe. Sometimes we believe the truth, and sometimes we believe lies." To finish her tree diagram, Grace wrote "Truth" under one root and "Lies" under the other.

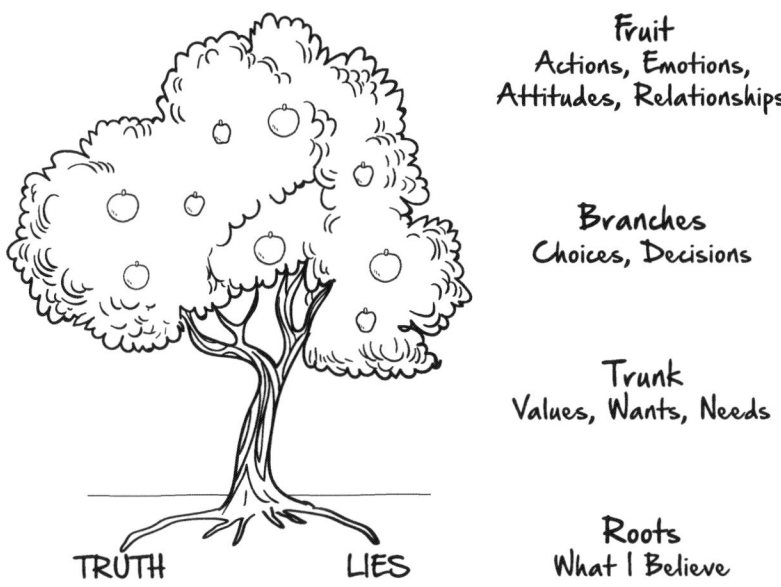

Grace picked up her phone again and opened her Bible app to Colossians 2:7 (NLT): "Let your roots grow down into Him, and let your lives be built on Him. Then your faith will grow strong in the truth you were taught, and you will overflow with thankfulness."

Grace sat back and examined her drawings, then summarized what God was showing her:

We start with lies or truth (roots), each leading into our core needs or values (trunk) that drive our decisions (branches), which ultimately determines the type of fruit our lives will bear. So if we want to bear good fruit, we not only need to make different decisions, but we also need to examine our belief systems and whether they are built on truth or lies.

HEALING GRACE: Practical Steps to Producing Good Fruit by Replacing Lies with Truth

Grace shut her eyes, inhaling the fragrance of freshly mowed grass, and began her conversation with God.

*Lord, You are the way, the truth, and the life. Truth comes from You. When I believe the truth, good fruit is visible in my life. I also know lies come from Satan. He's the father of lies. He tries to plant lies in my life through the things I see, hear, and experience. When I believe his lies, it produces rotten fruit in my life. Thank You for revealing the lie, showing me how to remove it, and replacing it with Your truth!*

As Grace choked out the last line, she thought maybe—just maybe—she saw the gnome tip his hat to her and smile.

MEETING MAXIMUS

*Chapter 3*

# MEETING MAXIMUS

*Are any of you sick? You should call for the elders of the church to come and pray over you, anointing you with oil in the name of the Lord. Such a prayer offered in faith will heal the sick, and the Lord will make you well. James 5:14–15 (NLT)*

The phone rang and rang until Grace's head finally emerged from under her feather pillow. Half asleep, she mumbled into the receiver, "Apples, pears, and plums."

"What?! Did I wake you up? Bless your heart," came her mother's voice.

As if brought to life by a double shot of espresso, Grace exclaimed, "Mom, sorry! Are you okay? What's up?"

"My doctor's appointment, young lady! Did you forget you're supposed to take me?"

Grace sprang from the bed in a panic and sent her phone flying into the air. Her hands slapped at it clumsily like a pizza-parlor trainee tossing dough for the first time. As she scrambled to spare the phone from hitting and shattering on the wood floors, she heard her mom shout, "Don't worry, Grace. The appointment isn't until ten this morning. You've got four hours to get ready." The call, the phone, and Grace's mouth dropped as she did the math. *6:00 A.M.? Mom!*

HEALING GRACE: Practical Steps to Producing Good Fruit by Replacing Lies with Truth

Slowly and gingerly, Grace's mom, Lizzie, struggled to haul her right leg into the car. Letting go of the car door, Grace reached down and gently tried to help her mother, but the movement evoked a soft groan.

"Sorry, Mom. I'm glad you're seeing the doctor today."

Lizzie didn't seem to notice Grace had spoken. She looked around and asked, "Where's your boyfriend? I thought he was supposed to drive us?"

"We broke up over six months ago," Grace chided, then shoved the passenger door shut.

As she walked around to the driver's side, her mom made sure she could still hear her assessment. "You never hold on to a guy, Grace."

As Grace buckled in, her mom looked her over from head to toe and offered a suggestion. "Maybe you should do something different with your hair."

"Okay," Grace sighed. She knew her mom wasn't trying to be hurtful, but she felt a tightness in her chest. *Lord, give me patience. She doesn't realize the power of her tongue.*

The drive to the office consisted of Grace's mom rattling on about Millie, the best hairdresser in town. "Don't you remember going to her when you were little? You looked so cute."

"With that pixie cut? Mom, I really hated it."

Grace's mother began listing the virtues of short hair. "No tangles! Easy to style, and you could comb it yourself. Grace, remember her sign out front?"

"Turn Your Mop into a Turned-On Top!" Together they recited Millie's motto and laughed. Grace was grateful that the mood in the car began to lighten.

## MEETING MAXIMUS

Thanks to Grace's lead foot, they arrived at the medical office of Dr. Max Miracle fifteen minutes early. Grace chirped, "Wow, what a great name for a doctor! Is he a Christian, Mom?"

"Honey, I don't know. What a silly thing to ask! Oh, Grace, could you grab my water bottle? My mouth feels like the Sahara!"

After fishing her reading glasses out from the bottom of her purse, Lizzie worked on filling out the new patient intake forms. Grace stayed close to the reception counter in case her mom needed help, but turned to look around the waiting room. Several patients were watching a timeless episode of *The Andy Griffith Show* on a large TV screen attached to the back wall. She spotted several Bibles and Christian magazines scattered around. *Nice!*

"Stand up straight, Grace," barked her mom as she turned from the counter to take a seat. In Grace's rush to keep up, she stumbled over the leg of an abandoned walker. *Clumsy!* Grace noticed a kind, old gentleman smiling sympathetically. Performing an awkward twirl she teased, "You should see me on the dance floor!" Her new friend gave her a happy little wink.

Apparently enrolled in the aromatherapy program of "Antiseptic Bliss," the doctor's office was a germ graveyard. A bucket of bleach would have envied the sanitizing scent. Grace whipped out her phone for a breath of fresh news and social media antics.

When the door leading to the exam rooms opened and her mother's name was called, Grace tucked her phone into her purse and reached for her mom's elbow. She walked beside her down the hallway to Exam Room 3. After giving her mother a boost onto the paper-covered exam table, Grace sat down in one of the two orange metal chairs decorating the space.

"Honey, could you hand me a magazine? I'll look at it while we wait."

After selecting one of the newer copies of *Beautiful Homes* for her mom, Grace took inventory of the small room. There was a box of latex

15

gloves, a couple of glass jars filled with wooden tongue depressors and cotton balls, a brown pump bottle filled with alcohol, a paper towel dispenser, a blood pressure cuff, a wall-mounted otoscope for checking patient's ears, and a plastic display overflowing with health pamphlets.

"I hear someone whistling the Andy Griffith theme song," whispered her mother.

Before Grace could reply, she heard the clipboard with her mom's paperwork being lifted out of the slot on their exam door. As the door swung open to reveal Dr. Miracle, Grace hastily dropped the plastic heart model back onto the shelf and her mom wedged the magazine under her leg.

Grace's initial examination of the doctor included his height of six feet, his muscular build, his remarkably good looks, and his deep blue eyes. His dark hair was cut short on the sides and longer on top. Grace reached up to fluff her hair and realized a trip to good-old-Millie's wouldn't have been a bad idea after all.

"Good morning, Ms. Walker! I'm Dr. Max Miracle." He gently took Grace's mom by the hand and smiled kindly. Then he turned to acknowledge the other person in the room. "And who's this? I'm going out on a limb and guess this is your daughter."

"Yes, that's Grace, my youngest. She's single."

"Mo-ther!" Grace hissed through her teeth.

Dr. Miracle extended his hand again and looked intently into Grace's eyes.

Grace felt her face flush and could only manage a squeaky, "Hi." Dr. Miracle smiled and turned back to his patient.

*Get ahold of yourself, Grace. He's probably married with six kids! And if he isn't married, he's totally out of your league.*

Dr. Miracle looked over at Grace with an expression she couldn't quite identify.

## MEETING MAXIMUS

*Oh my gosh, did I say that out loud?*

Dr. Miracle chatted comfortably with his patient as he checked her eyes, ears, throat, blood pressure, and heart. He thoughtfully listened as Grace's mom described her eating habits and daily activities. He guided her through some general health questions.

As the interview became more and more specific, Grace listened with growing concern.

"Have you had any trouble with your vision lately? Any blurriness?" asked Dr. Miracle.

"Yes, I think I need a new pair of reading glasses. I had trouble filling out your forms this morning. I think the print was too small. They really should be redone." Grace's eyebrows lifted at her mom's unsolicited advice.

Not bothered by her criticism, the doctor nodded as if that were a very good idea. "Okay. How about any pain or discomfort in your feet or legs, Ms. Walker?"

"No, I've been feeling pretty good. However, growing old isn't for sissies."

Grace gently interrupted, "Mom, you were in some pain this morning when you got into the car. Remember?"

With a tone of dismissal, she replied, "That's just from the sore on my leg. It's taking a long time to heal."

"You have a sore on your leg? Do you mind if I take a look?"

Alarmed, Grace leaned over to see around the table as her mother rolled up her pant leg, revealing a red, open wound. "Ms. Walker, tell me what happened?"

"I got up in the middle of the night to use the restroom, for about the tenth time, and bumped into my wooden footstool. It's a cute little thing. My father made it for me when I was around four or five. No, I was four because we were still living in the two-story house on Mass

# HEALING GRACE: Practical Steps to Producing Good Fruit by Replacing Lies with Truth

Street. I'd climb up on it to help my mother do the dishes. I loved washing dishes. I wish I still did." The memory brought a laugh.

The doctor smiled but continued his line of questions in a more serious tone. "How long has it been since your last blood test?"

"Why? Well, maybe years. I haven't seen a doctor in quite a while. I'm like my dad, healthy as a horse. He died years ago, diabetic complications."

"Alright, Ms. Walker, here's my concern. You seem to be experiencing some chronic symptoms caused by Type 2 Diabetes. The wound on your leg, your blurred vision, frequent urination, and diabetes in your family could be warning signs. I'm going to set you up at our local lab to get your bloodwork done. You'll need to be fasting for the test. It will give us a better picture of what your blood sugar has been doing over the past three months."

Grace noticed her mother had gone silent and her eyes were welling up with tears. She gently reached out and took her hand.

Dr. Miracle nodded and said, "But, Ms. Walker, here's what we're going to do first. I'm going to pray for you. Is that okay?"

Surprised by the doctor's offer, she questioned, "Right now?"

"Yes, ma'am!"

"I hope you don't expect me to kneel."

"No, you can stay right where you are."

Grace's mom nodded permission, and Dr. Miracle lightly touched her shoulder as he prayed, "Heavenly Father, I believe You still heal today. Your Word says by Jesus' stripes we are healed, so I ask You to heal Ms. Walker. Give her peace, faith to believe, and wisdom to make lifestyle changes. Let Your miraculous healing begin. In Jesus' name, amen."

Grace's mom looked up, wide-eyed, "You should have been a preacher instead of a doctor. That was a jim¬-dandy prayer!"

MEETING MAXIMUS

"You think so? Thank you, Ms. Walker! I gave it my best shot," he teased. "I want my relationship with the Lord to permeate every area of my life. I don't need a pulpit to share my faith. That notion may surprise the people who think they can 'compartmentalize' their life. They put their work in one box, relationships in another box, health in a box, and even their spiritual life in a box. But God wants to be involved in every area of my life, even my profession."

Lizzie nodded, and Dr. Miracle continued. "Do you mind if I demonstrate?" Lizzie nodded again, and he asked to take her hand. "It's easier to explain if I use your hand as a prop."

He gently held her wrist and explained, "Your wrist represents the spiritual area of life, your relationship with God. Just as your hand needs to be connected to your body to survive, you have to be connected to God to experience life. If you aren't connected to God, every area of your life will suffer. Wouldn't you agree?"

Grace piped up, "Absolutely!"

"Jesus said, 'Apart from Me, you can do nothing.' What do you think that means?"

Lizzie thought for a moment and replied, "Does it mean we can't do anything good without God?"

Dr. Miracle directed the question to Grace and waited for her to answer also.

She smiled, "I think it means apart from Him, I can do nothing. Even people who don't believe in God are still completely dependent upon Him for everything: the air they breathe, the food they eat—everything. Even if they don't realize it."

"Oh! Can I change my answer?" asked her mother.

The doctor grinned and continued his illustration by pointing to her mom's palm. "Your palm represents the soul—your thoughts, feelings, and decisions. They are influenced by your relationship with God."

Next, he tapped her thumb. "Your thumb represents the physical area of life." Pointing again at her palm, he stated, "As a doctor, I know our bodies are positively or negatively affected by how we think, feel, and decide." Tracing a path from her palm to her wrist, he added, "A healthy soul is connected to God. Remember, apart from Him, we can do nothing."

Grace leaned in with interest, and the doctor went on. "Your pointer finger represents the social area of life—your relationships with others. Your relationships are connected to and influenced by the palm and wrist. This example holds true of the remaining areas. The middle finger represents the financial area. The ring finger, the marital area, and the pinky, the parental area."

"Let me ask you this question," he continued. "What happens if you hurt just one part of your hand? Let's say you slam one of your fingers in a door. How does that injury affect the rest of your hand?"

"Everything hurts!" Grace and her mother chimed in together.

"The same is true in life," Dr. Miracle continued. "When one area suffers, every area is affected. The areas of life are connected, not compartmentalized."

"That's a great illustration, Dr. Miracle!" declared Grace.

"Call me Max, please."

"What?"

THE BOARDROOM

## Chapter 4

# THE BOARDROOM

*If two of you agree here on earth concerning anything you ask, My Father in heaven will do it for you. For where two or three gather together as My followers, I am there among them.*
Matthew 18:19–20 (NLT)

Grace swayed leisurely in her hammock, sorting through the emails on her phone. *Delete, delete, delete! Junk! Spam! Whoa! Wait a minute, this one isn't trash!* The subject line read, Good Fruit Ministry with Rhema and Shekinah Powers. *My friend, Shekinah! She's gotten remarried!* Grace quickly opened the email, expecting it to be an auto letter of some sort, but it was addressed to "My Sister Grace."

Grace threw her legs over either side of the hammock and sat up, rocking back and forth as she read.

So much has happened since I last saw you, Grace! God has blessed me with a wonderful Christian husband who is loving and kind to the twins. We're in ministry together! Sister, I couldn't be happier!

We started Good Fruit Ministry a few years ago, and God has caused it to grow beyond our wildest dreams. It is an online boardroom for people around the world who want to grow in the Lord and be taught by quality teachers. We gather virtually.

You touched my life in such a profound way. In fact, I don't think I would have been ready to meet and marry Rhema if you hadn't walked me through the process of forgiving my ex-husband. We'd like you to teach a couple of the Good Fruit boardroom 30-minute sessions.

If you're available, Rhema and I will start by greeting everyone and then introduce you. You'll be able to see the participants, and they will be able to see you. The computer program we use includes a whiteboard screen for writing or drawing if you need it. Or you can draw on a flip chart and hold it up to the camera.

The next boardroom session is this Thursday. Are you available? Let me know.

Forever grateful,
Shekinah (Rhodes) Powers

Grace sprung up with enthusiasm, ready to dash into the house to respond with a resounding "Yes!" However, the Holy Spirit gently reigned in her excitement, and she slowed to a trot. Akin to a wise cowboy guiding a spirited horse homeward, the Holy Spirit brought to mind the verse Dr. Miracle had quoted earlier: "Apart from Me, you can do nothing."

Grace took a deep breath and then sat down at her desk, bowed her head, and prayed. *Thank you, Lord, for Shekinah! I'd love to teach one of their boardroom sessions. Is this an opportunity You are bringing me? I only want to do the good works You have prepared me to do.* Grace waited, and a beautiful peace swept over her. Tears filled her eyes, and she lifted her hands up. *I love You, Lord. I feel good about telling Shekinah and Rhema that I'll teach their boardroom session. One or more. Whatever You want.*

When she got up from her desk several hours later, Grace went over to the Freedom Wall and studied her photo of Shekinah. The woman in the picture smiled back at her. Her face was framed by high cheekbones and a crown of dark, braided hair. Her skin was rich, deep brown, smooth, and youthful. Although she was smiling, the faint lines around her eyes hinted at a much deeper story than was visible on the surface.

# THE BOARDROOM

Grace reached up and gently touched the picture. *Thank you, Lord, for touching her life!*

By Thursday, Shekinah and Rhema had explained to Grace the features of the teleconferencing platform they used. Shekinah looked regal as always. Her intricately braided hair was now adorned with colorful beads, forming an elegant crown atop her head. Her husband sat next to her, his hair close-cropped and peppered with grey. Grace noted with approval that his face was both strong and kind.

As people joined the virtual boardroom, they were warmly greeted by their hosts. As the names and faces of the attendees popped up on her computer screen, Grace studied each one, offering a silent prayer as God brought the words to her heart.

She spotted Shekinah's twin teen daughters, Trinity and D'Zion. *Thank You, Lord, for blessing those young ladies, she thought. Oh, there's Liri and her husband, Cliff. God, You are so good!* She grew increasingly excited about the message God had put on her heart.

The online class was attended by participants coming from a delightful mishmash of backgrounds, ethnicities, ages, and hairstyles that could rival the many fabulous posters in Millie's Beauty Salon. From silver foxes to rainbow-colored coifs, Grace couldn't help but chuckle at the unexpected gallery of diversity that God had assembled. There were couples, individuals, and a church group from North Carolina. She noticed one attendee joining the session via phone, so there was no name or picture. *Probably a bad hair day*, she mused.

With a well-planned script and accompanied by an exciting musical theme song, Rhema and Shekinah opened their meeting. "Welcome brothers and sisters to the Good Fruit Ministry Boardroom! We're your hosts, Shekinah and Rhema Powers!" Shekinah spoke with infectious enthusiasm. "Remember, whoever you are, wherever you are, whatever you have or don't have, God is calling you into a relationship with Him so you bear good fruit!"

As the music faded out, Shekinah smiled and announced, "We have a special guest with us today, Dr. Grace Walker! Grace is a biblical counselor here in Texas. The truths she is about to share from God's Word changed my life. Now she's going to share them with you! It's a privilege to have her join us in the boardroom. Welcome, Grace!"

Grace waved and inaudibly spoke, "It's great to be here!" Shekinah quickly interrupted to remind her to unmute.

Anxiously, Grace searched the screen for the correct icon. *Lord, help me! Phew, there it is.*

"Thank you, Shekinah! It's a real joy to be here. I'm honored!" A gentle round of applause was provided by Shekinah, Rhema, and several others.

Grace rubbed her palms together like a gymnast preparing to mount the uneven bars. "Okay! Let's jump right into one of the most important skills we need for being a victorious Christian. How do we win at life? The Bible lays out a very clear and practical blueprint to follow. It begins with making good decisions!

"Speaking of decisions, did you know it's estimated that the average adult makes more than 35,000 decisions per day?"

Satisfied by the look of surprise on several faces in the virtual boardroom, Grace proceeded. "Some of those decisions are small, like 'What time should I get out of bed this morning?' or 'Should I try a new flavor of coffee creamer?' Others are much larger, like 'How do I handle this conflict?' or 'Should I take this job?'"

Grace noted several of the faces on the screen nodding. "Let's pray together and ask God to speak to us as we get started."

Heads bowed, some from across the city and others across the world. "Heavenly Father, open our hearts and minds to Your Word," Grace began. "Teach us how to make good decisions—decisions that are made Your way and not our own. In Jesus' name, amen."

## THE BOARDROOM

There was a soft chorus of "amens," which Grace followed with a few instructions about grabbing a pen and paper for note taking and drawing a diagram.

"I'd like everyone to turn to Deuteronomy 30:19 (NLT), please. It has a lot to tell us about decision making."

Grace watched as participants opened their Bibles or reached for their phones to locate the verse. As she waited, audio picked up a dog barking and children laughing in one of the participants' backgrounds. She smiled as a tabby cat gazed into another of the participants' cameras until being gently swatted out of the way. A couple attendees looked confused, however, prompting Shekinah to repeat the reference and explain that it was in the fifth book of the Bible.

When most of the group had located the verse, Grace began, "Follow along with me, 'Today I have given you the choice between life and death, between blessings and curses. Now I call on heaven and earth to witness the choice you make. Oh, that you would choose life, so that you and your descendants might live!'"

Grace surveyed the patchwork of faces on the screen and began, "It's true that our lives are filled with choices and decisions. We decide everything from what to eat to whom to marry. This verse in Deuteronomy clearly states that every choice is a crossroads. But which way will we go? Based on what we decide, one path leads to life and the other path leads to death."

Grace directed a question to everyone in the boardroom. "Raise your hand if you think God is interested in every decision you make." A couple of members waved wildly, three gave a thumbs-up, and several looked unsure. One simply crossed her arms.

"Rhema, what do you think? Do you think God cares about every decision we make?"

Rhema looked thoughtful, then responded, "Absolutely! We don't know how our decisions will affect ourselves, others, or our future.

That's why we must be directed by God, even in what we consider to be 'small' decisions."

"Good answer, Rhema! Thank you for letting me pick on you! Since our decisions lead to life or death, it's important to know how to make good decisions."

Grace was drowned out by a participant identified as Asani. "What about freewill and intelligence?" she demanded. "Do we really need to ask God about everything? I don't think it's as important as you're making it."

Grace paused for a split second to ask God for wisdom. "Asani, I appreciate your question. Tell us a little about yourself. Where are you from, and I'm curious about your name?"

Asani clearly had been expecting a fight, not a gracious response, and Grace noticed a tiny crack appear in her rough exterior. Even so, her guard was lowered only a smidgen, like the window of a driver caught speeding cautiously engaging in a conversation with a traffic cop.

Asani continued with a spirited declaration, "I call myself 'Asani,' which is Swahili for 'rebellious.' I'm an independent woman from Kenya. So what's your take on that?"

The virtual room hung in suspense, waiting for Grace's response to this bold introduction.

"Are you currently living in Kenya, Asani?" Grace asked. "It looks like you might be in a dorm room." Grace thought she heard a chuckle from one of the participants in the background.

Asani stiffened. "I'm in the US right now. I'm a Behavioral Science major at Southern University."

Grace leaned forward and addressed Asani in a gentle tone, "How interesting! Thank you for sharing a little bit about yourself. I like your question, 'Since God gave us freewill, why do we need to ask Him about every decision we make?' Is that what you are asking?"

## THE BOARDROOM

"Right! God gave us a brain. He expects us to use it," Asani added.

Deciding to enlist the other boardroom members, Grace queried, "Anyone have a Scripture that might shed some light on Asani's question?"

The boardroom went silent for a couple of seconds and then several hands went up.

Shekinah unmuted Nasimul (Nash) from Bangladesh, who spoke slowly, trying to articulate each word clearly. "I think of Proverbs 3:5, which says, 'Trust in the LORD with all your heart, and lean not on your own understanding.' That verse really speaks to me, because I tend to spend hours trying to figure out how to handle a problem without asking God first. That is me leaning on my own understanding. But!"– Nasimul raised his pointer finger as if a lightbulb had come on–"the moment I come to Jesus and ask Him for help, the answer becomes crystal clear. Often, He shows me to go in a direction I would never have thought of."

"Thank you, Nash! Let's have one more person share. How about you, Onn?"

Grace found herself captivated by the vibrant garden that formed the backdrop of Onn's virtual space as she responded, "In John 5:30 (NLT), Jesus modeled how we are to live," she said, gently touching her necklace, on which hung both a cross and the Star of David. "He explained, 'I can do nothing on my own.' How much more should we consult with Him before any action? How much should I budget for groceries? Let me consult with my Father. Should I go to the party I was invited to after work? Let me consult with my Father. Should I work in this ministry or serve in another way? Let me consult with my Father."

"Thank you, Nasimul and Onn! Sometimes, a decision doesn't matter, and God is okay with whatever you decide. The point is you won't know unless you ask. By asking, you are putting God's will first."

Grace noted that for someone who had just self-identified as rebellious, Asani was oddly quiet. "What do you think, Asani?" Grace spoke with a softness in her voice that widened the crack in Asani's wall.

"Yeah, it makes sense. By not asking God for direction or like Nash said, 'leaning on my own understanding,' my life has been one disaster after another. My parents barely have anything to do with me." Asani thought for a moment and continued, "They are paying for my education, but I didn't once consult God about going to college, and if He wanted me to go, which one to choose. Now, everything I'm learning at university goes contrary to what we're talking about. Bottom line, this is an area I obviously need help in," she confessed.

With a gentle smile, Grace offered support. "Let's take this step by step. You've already taken the first step by recognizing the need for God's guidance. Prayerfully consider seeking His wisdom in each decision, allowing Him to direct your steps. You're not alone in this journey. God is always ready to guide and walk alongside you." She concluded warmly, "If you're comfortable, I'd love to pray for you and your journey ahead. May God grant you the wisdom, clarity, and peace as you seek His guidance in all aspects of your life."

Grace bowed her head in prayer, inviting the class to join in seeking God's guidance and wisdom for Asani. Her prayer was short and heartfelt. "Thank You, Lord, for Asani! We pray for her to hear Your voice clearly and follow You more and more each day. Touch her right now. We ask that You give her wisdom and clarity as she seeks Your will for her life. In Jesus' name, amen."

When Grace opened her eyes, she almost had to look twice. *Lord, is Asani crying?* "Bless you, Asani!"

Grace then turned her gaze to the rest of the participants in the boardroom. "We all need God's help in making good decisions, don't we?" she continued. "So how about I share with y'all a practical and effective way to start making more good decisions and fewer bad ones?" Grace's Texas twang peeked through for a second, briefly causing several of the participants to descend into peals of laughter. "There are seven different areas of life that require decisions. If you are taking notes, this might be a good place to take them."

Raising her fingers as she itemized each area, Grace enumerated the following list:

- **The Spiritual Area:** your relationship with God.
- **The Psychological Area:** your mind, will, and emotions.
- **The Social Area:** your relationships with others.
- **The Physical Area:** your body.
- **The Financial Area:** your money.
- **The Marital Area:** your relationship with your spouse (if you are married).
- **The Parental Area:** your relationship with your children (if you have children).

"Every day, we make decisions in one or more of those areas, and one decision might overlap into several others," Grace continued. "I'll illustrate the art of decision making by drawing a simple diagram, which I'd like you to draw with me." *Let's see if I remember how to use the boardroom's whiteboard*, Grace softly mumbled to herself. She clicked on the whiteboard icon to share her screen with the participants. She chose the black pen icon and began to draw a couple of lines and then wrote in the areas of life.

```
Spiritual
Psychological
Social
Physical
Financial
Marital
Parental
```

Heads were bobbing up and down as they glanced back and forth from the screen to their drawing. "I've listed the seven areas of life. Each of those areas of life generates its own set of needs, problems, and questions."

Grace sketched a rough arrow and filled it with the words "needs," "problems," "questions."

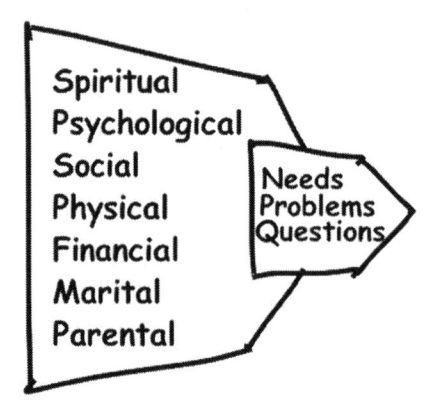

```
┌─────────────────┐
│ Spiritual       │╲
│ Psychological   │ ╲
│ Social          │  ┌─────────╲
│ Physical        │  │ Needs    ╲
│ Financial       │  │ Problems  >
│ Marital         │  │ Questions╱
│ Parental        │  └─────────╱
│                 │ ╱
└─────────────────┘╱
```

"Those needs, problems, and questions lead us to the point of having to make one or more decisions." Grace added a circle labeled "decisions" to her illustration.

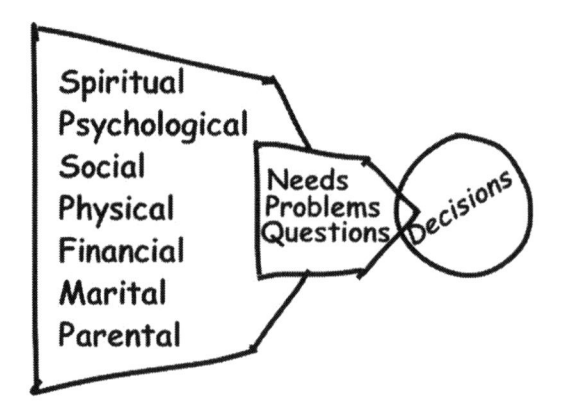

```
┌─────────────────┐
│ Spiritual       │╲
│ Psychological   │ ╲
│ Social          │  ┌─────────╲  ╭──────╮
│ Physical        │  │ Needs    ╲ │      │
│ Financial       │  │ Problems  >│Decisions│
│ Marital         │  │ Questions╱ │      │
│ Parental        │  └─────────╱  ╰──────╯
│                 │ ╱
└─────────────────┘╱
```

## THE BOARDROOM

Grace evaluated her drawing so far and announced, "As you *can* see, I've set the artistic bar very high!" She heard chuckles from a few unmuted participants.

"Decision time! Your decision will lead to one of two places: life or death." Grace added arrows, ovals, and text to her diagram.

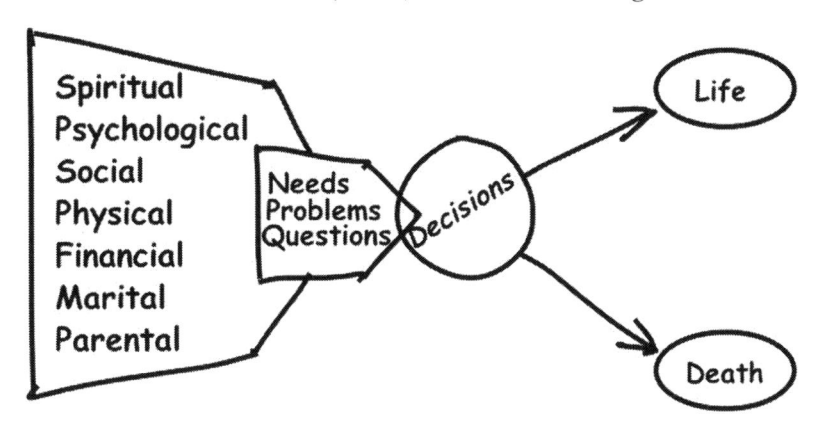

```
Spiritual
Psychological
Social         Needs
Physical       Problems   Decisions  →  Life
Financial      Questions
Marital                              →  Death
Parental
```

"As you look at this diagram, consider our verse in Deuteronomy: 'Today I have given you the choice, or decision, between life and death. . . . Oh, that you would choose life!'" As she recited the verse, she traced the diagram with the pointer feature for emphasis. "God wants us to choose life."

"Dr. Grace, excuse me for interrupting. This is Abram in Pakistan."

"Yes, Abram, go ahead."

"What does 'choose life' mean? Is this about heaven?"

"Great question!" said Grace. "Choosing life can be about our decision to receive Jesus as our Savior, which leads to heaven, but it also means choosing to follow God daily, which results in His blessings." Grace wrote "Spirit" on the arrow pointing to the life oval.

Onn piped up, "And 'choosing death'?"

"The path leading to death is about living independent of God's direction and prioritizing my own desires. My way ultimately leads to negative consequences. The inclination toward self-serving behavior is often referred to as the 'flesh' in the Bible." Grace wrote "flesh" on the path leading downward toward death.

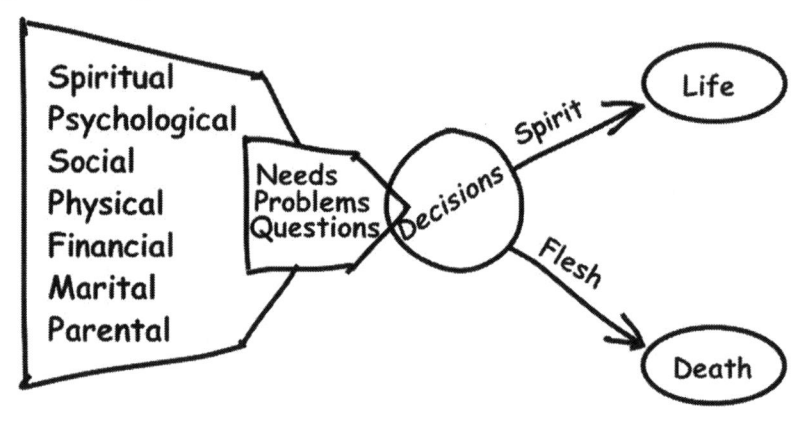

*Spiritual, Psychological, Social, Physical, Financial, Marital, Parental → Needs, Problems, Questions → Decisions → Spirit → Life / Flesh → Death*

Quickly interjecting a Scripture that came to her mind, Shekinah quoted Proverbs 14:12: "There is a way that seems right to a man, but its end is the way of death."

"Exactly!" Grace exclaimed. "Although the path of the flesh may seem enticing (or even the right one to take at times), Shekinah just reminded us of the truth found in Proverbs 14, verse 12." Grace noticed several participants jotting down the Scripture reference and repeated its location.

"I call this 'taking the Flesh Freeway,' and ultimately it costs us. It leads to pain and suffering for us and those around us. Do any of you have a personal example of getting on this road?"

Grace prompted the participants to share their experiences. Soon, there was a lively discussion. One gentleman's video froze midsentence, and the participants burst into laughter as they realized he had been stuck in a hilarious expression for several minutes. Grace couldn't help but join in the mirth, turning the awkward situation into a lighthearted moment.

Grace moved on with a smile. "You will experience life or death based on your decisions. What would be an example of experiencing life in the financial area of life?"

Lovejoy in Nigeria unmuted and responded. Grace admired his deep baritone voice. "If you follow the Spirit regarding your money and job, the *life* you might experience is having enough to meet your needs and the needs of others."

"That's right, Lovejoy, and the death you may experience could be what?" Grace queried.

"Hmm, perhaps debt, worry, and loss."

"Right! I have another verse we can read. Who would like to read Romans 8:6 (NASB) for us? First one to find it, go ahead."

There was a moment of silence with Abram in Pakistan locating the verse first. "I have it, ma'am. 'For the mind set on the flesh is death, but the mind set on the Spirit is life and peace.'"

"If you've experienced death in any of these areas because of bad decisions, wave at me." Grace laughed as everyone, including herself waved. "Right! We all have. I don't think anyone intends to make decisions that end in death, but that's what happens when you follow your flesh. Our way *seems* right in the moment, or we wouldn't choose it. Someone look up and read Galatians 6:8."

Abram again got there first and read, "For he who sows to his flesh will of the flesh reap corruption, but he who sows to the Spirit will of the Spirit reap everlasting life."

Grace pointed to the corresponding parts of the diagram as he read.

"Thank you, Abram! This verse also illustrates how our decisions lead to either life or death. Since all of us want to experience life and avoid death, it's important to recognize what our flesh wants—identifying its motivation. Let's add to our diagram a list of possible motives behind deciding to follow the flesh instead of the Spirit."

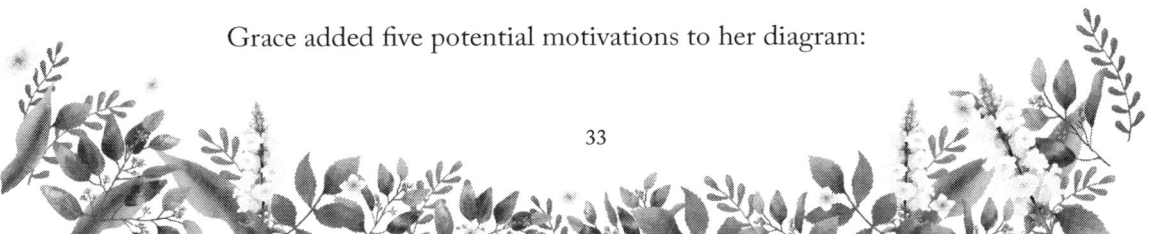

Grace added five potential motivations to her diagram:

- Selfishness
- Pride
- Vanity
- Defending my rights
- Fear

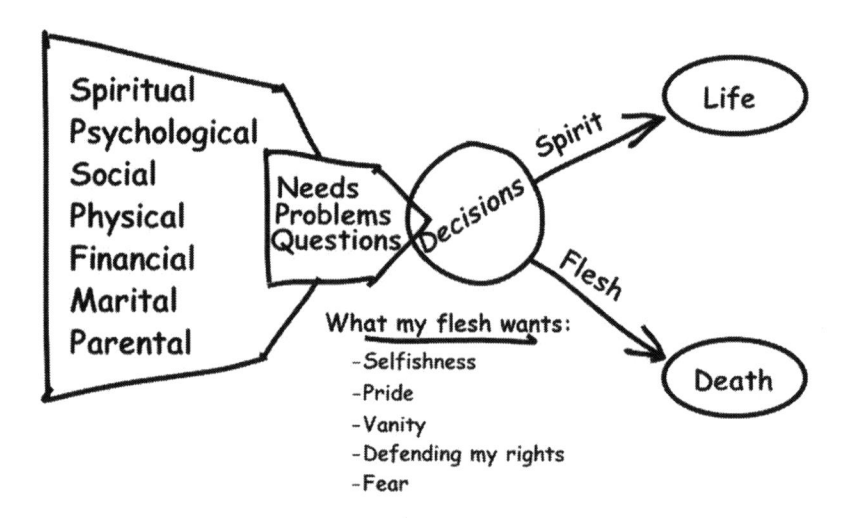

[Diagram: Spiritual, Psychological, Social, Physical, Financial, Marital, Parental → Needs, Problems, Questions → Decisions → Spirit → Life; Flesh → Death. What my flesh wants: -Selfishness, -Pride, -Vanity, -Defending my rights, -Fear]

Again, heads nodded up and down as they copied the list. "Shall we unpack these terms? Think about a poor decision you made recently. Which fleshly motivation was behind your decision?"

Grace tried to identify what the various members were feeling based on some of their facial expressions. She wasn't sure if it was apprehension, embarrassment, or some other emotion, but all eyes were focused on the screen, including the tabby cat sitting on Lexi's shoulder in Colorado.

"Was selfishness behind your decision? Selfishness often drives our decisions as we prioritize our own desires, possessions, time, or comfort above all else. For example, perhaps we choose not to help someone in need, because it would inconvenience us. I think, this is *my* life, *my* body, *my* money, and *my* time."

Sig, joining from Canada, squirmed in his seat and avoided eye contact.

"Or was your decision motivated by pride? Pride will motivate us to rely on our own abilities or intellect, disregarding guidance or wisdom from God or others: 'leaning on our own understanding.' We think we are better than others or we want to be independent and not need anyone." Lexi bit her lip and appeared introspective. Asani lifted up her notebook to cover her face.

Grace continued. "Here's another motivation: vanity. Making decisions rooted in vanity might involve seeking recognition, admiration, or attention. This could be seen in choosing activities or making choices based on how we will look to others."

Grace looked quickly at the faces on the screen, continuing to try to gauge their reactions, then moved on quickly.

"How about defending your rights? That's another big one. Was your decision motivated by defending your right to do something you think you have a right to do? Decisions influenced by defending one's rights often stem from a sense of entitlement, believing we deserve certain treatment or privileges. This might result in doing or saying things to assert *our* perceived rights, but what happens when our rights infringe upon the rights of others? What if insisting on *my* rights means trampling on the needs, desires, and rights of someone else?"

The participants appeared engrossed, their brows furrowed in concentration. Grace could hear the sound of scratching as they eagerly took notes.

"Here's a pop quiz. When was the last time you caught yourself thinking that you had a right to be treated a certain way or get certain things?" Based on the sheepish looks on many of the participants' faces, Grace grinned. "That's what I thought! Lastly, another powerful motivation is fear. Fear puts us on this downward path." Grace pointed to the diagram and traced the route leading to death.

"Making a decision based on any of these motives may seem right at the time, but they lead to death because we are following our flesh." Grace paused for her words to hit home. "Does anyone want to share the motivation behind one of your poor decisions?"

Onn spoke up first. "I've been struggling to make ends meet after I quit my job. God just showed me that my decision to quit my job was motived by two things, fear and demanding my rights. I suffer from anxiety, and because I was afraid of being around everyone in our small office space, I expected them to let me work from home. When they wouldn't, I quit. I haven't been able to find a job since."

"Thank you for sharing, Onn. Let me ask you, did you pray about whether you should quit your job?"

"Hmmm, I don't think I did," Onn confessed.

"Right. Jesus gave us His example to follow. Listen to Philippians 2:5–7 (NLT): 'You must have the same attitude that Christ Jesus had. Though He was God, He did not think of equality with God as something to cling to. Instead, He gave up His divine privileges.' In other words, Jesus did not *demand* or cling to His *rights* as God.' What does that verse teach us?"

Lovejoy spoke softly, "To humble ourselves like Jesus. Follow His example."

"Exactly! He never made His decisions based on selfishness, pride, vanity, fear, or the need to defend His rights. Philippians 2:3 (NLT) says, 'Don't be selfish; don't try to impress others. Be humble, thinking of others as better than yourselves.'—that's pride. What other verse comes to mind when you think of pride?"

Nasimul waved to answer. Grace nodded for him to go ahead. "Proverbs 16:18 says, 'Pride goes before destruction, and a haughty spirit before a fall.' That sounds like the path to death on the diagram, Dr. Grace."

"You're right, it sure does, Nash! What Scripture talks about not being motived by fear?"

# THE BOARDROOM

After peeling her tabby off her shoulder, Lexi unmuted. "I think of 2 Timothy 1:7. 'For God has not given us a spirit of fear, but of power and of love and of a sound mind.'"

"Great verse, Lexi! Thanks!"

Rhema spoke up and announced, "It's time for a quick break, Grace. Now that we've talked about how easily we can make poor decisions, let's look forward to sharing how to make good decisions. Dr. Grace will do that when we come back in five minutes."

Grace exhaled as if she'd been holding her breath the whole time. She gave a nod.

Rhema muted everyone while they grabbed a drink or stretched. Grace ran to grab a glass of water, and while she was near the bathroom, she ducked in to brush her hair. When she looked in the mirror, she grimaced. There were a few flyaways she hadn't noticed. *I'll bet that looks good in my close-up video!* She tucked the misbehaving strands behind her ear and spritzed some hairspray to hold them in place. *There! Easy-peasy.*

Grace made her way back to her computer and saw that several of the participants were starting to filter back as well. After several more minutes, the majority of participants were back in front of their cameras. Rhema unmuted himself.

"Welcome back!" he said. "I hope you all had a refreshing break! As a reminder, we have our special guest, Dr. Grace Walker, with us. We have been talking about how making decisions based on what our flesh wants leads to death. Sometimes that death is physical, but more often, it's metaphorical of the negative consequences we will experience. Now that we've talked about decisions leading to death, we'll move on to the fun stuff. Grace, please share with us the three keys to making good decisions that lead to life!"

Grace smiled and spoke, "Happy to, Rhema! We learned what our flesh wants, but we need to know what God wants! The first key to making a good decision is understanding that God wants us to trust

Him with everything. That includes all of our needs." Grace used her virtual marker to add the heading "What God Wants" followed by "Trust God."

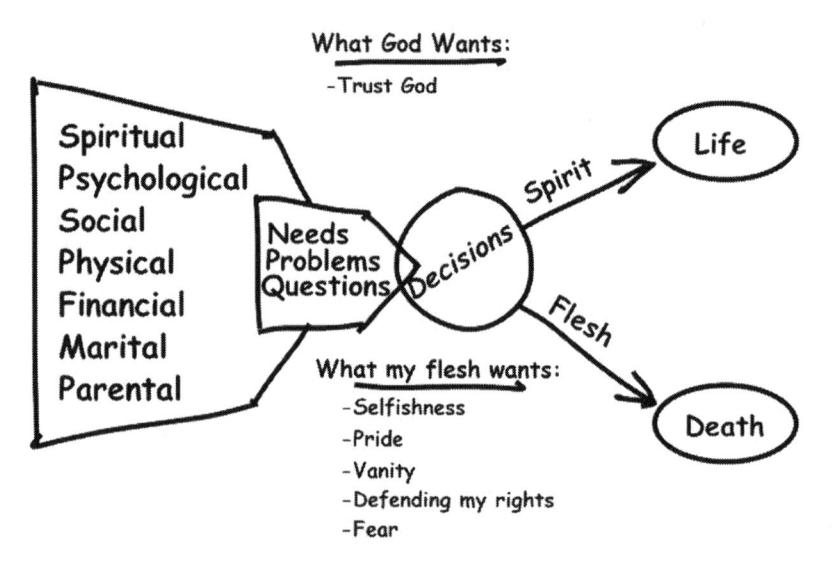

**What God Wants:**
- Trust God

Spiritual
Psychological
Social
Physical
Financial
Marital
Parental

Needs
Problems
Questions

Decisions

Spirit → Life

Flesh → Death

**What my flesh wants:**
- Selfishness
- Pride
- Vanity
- Defending my rights
- Fear

"Unfortunately, sometimes we rush ahead, trying to meet our own needs before trusting God first. We get impatient or forget how good He is."

Grace called on Lovejoy to read Philippians 4:19. Again, his rich baritone voice resonated through the screen: "And my God shall supply all your need according to His riches in glory by Christ Jesus."

"Thank you! Trusting God is learning to wait on God to meet your needs. God is waiting for you to trust Him. I love this verse in Isaiah 30:18 (NLT). It says, 'So the Lord must wait for you to come to Him so He can show you His love and compassion. For the Lord is a faithful God. Blessed are those who wait for His help.' A good question to ask yourself is, Am I waiting on God to meet my needs or am I getting impatient and trying to do His job for Him?"

## THE BOARDROOM

Grace paused and turned to her hosts. "Shekinah, do you ever get impatient for God to meet your needs? At times, I know I do," she confessed.

Shekinah unmuted her microphone and acknowledged there were many times after her divorce that she had grown impatient with God, but as she trusted Him and waited, He was faithful to bring her Rhema. She continued, "A lot of times, we make decisions just so we don't have to wait. Like Abraham and Sarah, they got tired of waiting for God to give them a son, so what did they do? They decided to take things into their own hands. At Sarah's urging, Abraham fathered a child, Ishmael, with Sarah's handmaid, Hagar. That one decision not only brought many problems into every area of their lives, but also continues to have ripple effects in the world today."

Many of the participants looked quizzical. Onn raised her hand. "What do you mean?"

Shekinah nodded. "How many of you know that all the fighting between Israel and the Arab nations can be traced back to this one decision?" Several of the participants raised their eyebrows. "That's right! The people of Israel are the descendants of Isaac, the son of Abraham and Sarah, while the Arab people are descendants of Ishmael. That's why there is so much fighting, because there is a disagreement over who the land belongs to. Abraham and Sarah got impatient, and that region of the world has been fighting ever since."

"Thank you, Shekinah!" Grace interjected. "This is such a good lesson for all of us that God knows the best plan and the best timing. When we try to get ahead of God, we can really mess things up. Ephesians 3:20 (NLT) says, 'He [God] is able to accomplish infinitely more than we might ask or think.' So why wouldn't we want to trust Him with everything, even when His plan takes longer than we expect? Speaking of which . . ." Grace brought up her drawing on the whiteboard. "Time to add the second key to our diagram. What does God want us to do with problems while we're waiting on His solution? He wants us to THANK HIM!"

# HEALING GRACE: Practical Steps to Producing Good Fruit by Replacing Lies with Truth

**What God Wants:**
- Trust God
- Thank God

Spiritual
Psychological
Social
Physical
Financial
Marital
Parental

Needs
Problems
Questions

Decisions

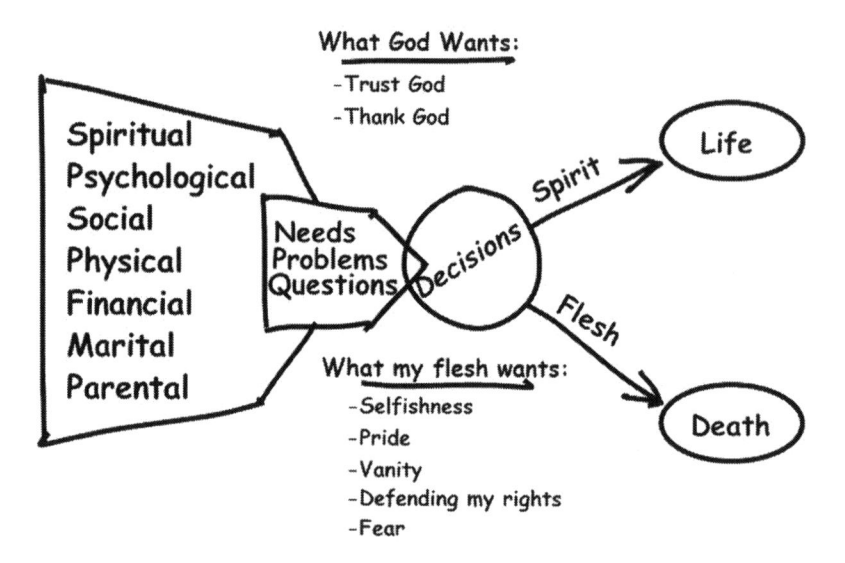

Spirit → Life

Flesh → Death

**What my flesh wants:**
- Selfishness
- Pride
- Vanity
- Defending my rights
- Fear

"What do you think of this verse in 1 Thessalonians 5:18?" Grace asked. "From the New Living Translation, it says, 'Be thankful in *all* circumstances, for this is God's will for you who belong to Christ Jesus.'"

Shekinah chimed in, "Another Scripture that comes to mind is Ephesians 5:20: 'Giving thanks always for *all* things to God the Father in the name of our Lord Jesus Christ.'"

Rhema added, "I've learned that thanking God for the things I like is simply good manners. However, when I thank God in *all* things, even the things I don't like, it proves I am trusting Him."

Asani waved her hand wildly and jumped in, "Thank God for even the bad things that happen to us? Are we supposed to thank Him for those?"

Grace responded, "The verse in 1 Thessalonians and the one Shekinah quoted both use the word 'all.' What does 'all' mean to you, Asani?"

She cocked her head and answered uncertainly, "I guess everything, good or bad?"

"Right! Thank Him for *all* things—good or bad—because no matter what we're going through, He is faithful and worthy of our praise."

Nasimul raised his hand and spoke, "Romans 8:28 also uses the word 'all.' It says, 'And we know that all things work together for good to those who love God, to those who are the called according to His purpose.'"

In a loving and fatherly tone, Rhema added, "Sometimes, situations that seem terrible at first can later be understood as part of a greater plan for good. By trusting Him and thanking Him in advance, we acknowledge that He promises to work through any circumstance—even the most difficult ones. We need to trust Him enough to believe that, ultimately, He will turn everything for good, even if we can't see it right away."

"That's right!" exclaimed Grace. "God promises to take the good *and* the bad things we experience and work them together for good. Let's choose to thank Him in *all* things and for *all* things."

Pointing at the diagram, Grace summarized the point. "When we experience problems, instead of complaining or getting depressed, we can choose to look to our good Heavenly Father and thank Him instead."

Onn held up her pointer finger to indicate she had something to add. "When we focus on our problems, they appear overwhelming, and God seems far away. But when we focus on God, we realize there is nothing too difficult for Him to handle or work together for good."

Grace gave Onn a quick thumbs-up. "Yes, nothing is too difficult for God. He wants us to trust Him with our needs and thank Him for our problems!"

Grace scribbled a few more words on her illustration. "Now . . . how about when we have questions? Check out what I've added to the diagram. Key 3 is to 'Ask God.'" She tapped the screen to enlarge the drawing so everyone could see.

**Diagram:**

Categories (Spiritual, Psychological, Social, Physical, Financial, Marital, Parental) → Needs, Problems, Questions → Decisions

- Spirit → Life
- Flesh → Death

**What God Wants:**
- Trust God
- Thank God
- Ask God

**What my flesh wants:**
- Selfishness
- Pride
- Vanity
- Defending my rights
- Fear

---

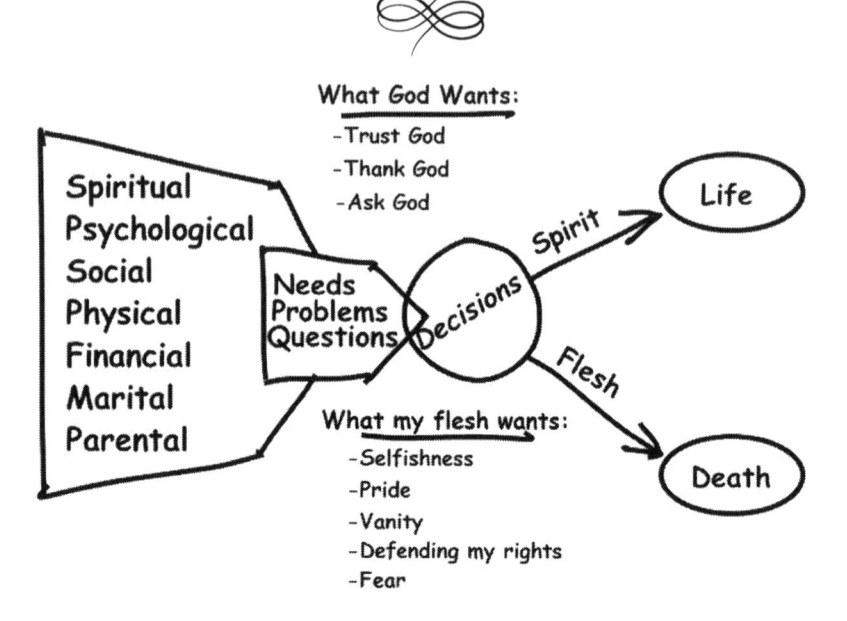

"Sometimes I don't know what to do because I haven't asked God what His will is," Grace continued. "James 1:5 (NLT) says, 'If you need wisdom, ask our generous God, and He will give it to you. He will not rebuke you for asking.' When you acknowledge God in every area of your life, He will show you what to do. Does anyone have Proverbs 3:5–6 memorized? Unmute yourself and share it."

There was a mad rush to unmute, and numerous voices shouted out, "Trust in the LORD with *all* your heart, and lean not on your own understanding; in *all* your ways acknowledge Him, and He shall direct your paths."

Grace laughed at the enthusiastic response and their noticeable emphasis on "all" as they recited the verses. "Well done! We face life or death decisions every day. We'll experience life when we follow the Holy Spirit and do what He shows us to do."

# THE BOARDROOM

## Life or Death Decisions

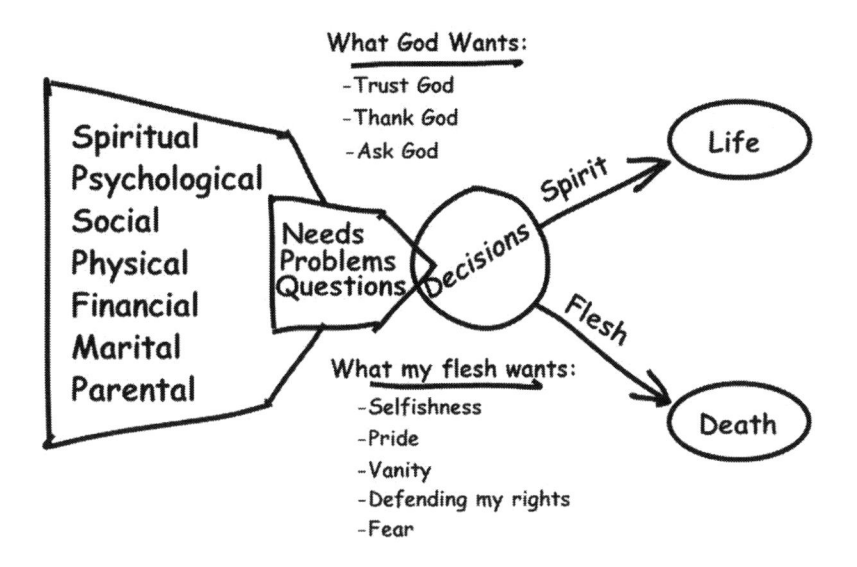

**What God Wants:**
- Trust God
- Thank God
- Ask God

Spiritual
Psychological
Social
Physical
Financial
Marital
Parental

Needs
Problems
Questions

Decisions

Spirit → Life

Flesh → Death

**What my flesh wants:**
- Selfishness
- Pride
- Vanity
- Defending my rights
- Fear

"It's time for me to wrap up our lesson. Who'd like to summarize it?"

"I will." The answer came from the male participant on the phone. "Grace, you shared how every decision leads to either life or death. We experience life when we choose to follow the Spirit. To do what God wants, we trust God with our needs, thank God for everything, even in the midst of our problems, and ask God for wisdom concerning our questions."

The voice was familiar, but Grace couldn't place it. She tilted her head as if it would help roll the identity of the speaker to the front of her mind. Suddenly realizing she needed to respond, she replied loudly, making a couple of participants jump, "Great summary! When you do those three things, you experience peace! Philippians 4:6–7 (NLT) says, 'Don't worry about anything; instead, pray about everything. Tell God what you need, and thank Him for *all* He has done. Then you will experience God's peace.'"

Shekinah quickly hopped in as Grace finished, thanking her for sharing such a practical and eye-opening lesson. "I want to see everyone's diagram. Hold it up for me."

Grace looked at each participant's masterpiece. Some drawings were huge and filled the whole page while others were tiny but neatly drawn. She smiled as she watched Shekinah's eyes study each diagram. "Great job, everyone! Let's invite Dr. Grace back next Thursday so we can share how this life lesson impacted us throughout the week."

The boardroom participants immediately responded with an amen, gestured with thumbs-up, virtually applauded, or used emojis to signify their thankfulness for learning the life skill of good decision-making.

Rhema joined in, "Okay, it's a plan! Grace will join us next week. Let me pray for you."

While the hosts closed the meeting, Grace marveled at how far God had taken Rhema and Shekinah and their ministry. When she tuned back in, they were signing off. "Thank you for joining us at the Good Fruit Ministry Boardroom today! Remember Jesus loves you. We love you, and God's got a good plan for your life!"

One by one the participants dropped off the screen. Shekinah spoke up, "Grace, I hope we didn't put you on the spot. Can you join us next week?"

"I'd love to, my friend! I can't wait to hear how God uses this message in people's lives!" They thanked her and clicked off before she could ask, "Who called in on the phone?"

## Chapter 5

# THE BOARDROOM FOLLOW-UP

*Then the way you live will always honor and please the Lord, and your lives will produce every kind of good fruit. All the while, you will grow as you learn to know God better and better.*
Colossians 1:10 (NLT)

---

Grace set up her lights, background, notes, and computer, and waited for the boardroom to begin.

As before, people were greeted by Rhema and Shekinah as they logged in. Grace recognized several of the participants from last week—Lexi and her cat, Nasimul, Onn, Sig, and others. Again, there was one attendee joining the session via phone with no name listed.

The theme song started right on the hour and the hosts announced, "Welcome brothers and sisters to the Good Fruit Ministry Boardroom!"

Grace's thoughts went heavenward as she prayed for the participants and asked God to bless the time. The next thing she heard was Shekinah saying, "Dr. Grace Walker is back with us today! Welcome, Grace!"

Grace waved. "Hi, everyone! I see some familiar faces and a few new ones." She paused for effect, "Well, they are probably the same faces you've always had." That tickled a couple of the participants and garnered a nice hardy snort from someone off screen.

Grace smiled and began by asking if anyone from the previous week had a testimony about how the lesson impacted their decision-making.

There was a significant pause, then Lexi spoke up, "I found myself in a situation where my pride just about dictated a nasty reaction at work. Everyone knew there was a promotion coming, and I thought I was being considered. Then they picked a guy over me. I started to get really angry, but instead of letting my emotions take over, I remembered last week's lesson and made a conscious choice to trust God instead. I went back to my desk and began silently thanking Him for this job, even without the promotion, and how He had provided for our family. You know what happened? Just an hour later, my boss called me to his office. There, he unveiled a brand-new role crafted specifically with me in mind. Grace, if I'd responded in any other way, it's doubtful they would have offered me this new position."

Right on cue, Lexi's furry companion sauntered into view, emitting a melodious meow, punctuating her testimony and evoking cheerful smiles and laughter from the boardroom.

"Thank you for sharing, Lexi! That is awesome that God brought the decision diagram to your mind. You trusted God, and He brought about the unexpected. Anyone else want to share?"

Asani unmuted herself and began, "In a conversation with my mom this week, she told me to work harder at school so I could get a good job. I thought, 'What does she think I've been doing? She's always telling me what to do! I'll never prove I'm good enough to her.' I started seething. As I mopped the floor of my apartment that night, I kept saying, 'I hate you! I hate you!' Suddenly God spoke to me! He said, 'But she doesn't hate you, Adora.' I began to cry because God called me by my given name and not the name I call myself, Asani. He called me Adora, the beloved one. That's the name my parents gave me."

Asani brushed tears from her eyes and continued her story. "In such a loving way, God showed me my rebellion, independence, hate, pride . . . oh, yes, and how I've fought to defend my rights. I knew I needed to call my parents and ask for their forgiveness, but I was afraid of what

## THE BOARDROOM FOLLOW-UP

they would say. I pulled out my notes from last week and began to pray. I asked God to help me trust Him, and I immediately experienced peace—like I was on the path to life." She paused to blow her nose.

Grace started to thank her for sharing, but Asani quickly recovered. "Wait, it gets even better! I did talk with my parents and asked their forgiveness for my hateful attitudes, lack of appreciation, and rejection of their advice and wisdom. Guess what?! They immediately said, 'Of course, we forgive you. We love you, Adora!' Isn't that awesome! God used that lesson to bring life into that relationship!"

The boardroom erupted into applause, cheers, and rousing versions of "Praise the Lord!"

"I love the name Adora," Shekinah ventured. "Could we begin calling you that too?"

"Yes, please do! It will remind me of God's love . . . and my parents' love," sniffed Adora.

"Lexi and Adora, would you mind emailing me your photos? I have this special 'Freedom Wall' in my office where I hang snapshots of folks set free by the grace of God during our classes, letters, or one-on-one counseling sessions."

"My photo is there," piped up Shekinah.

"Yes, it is!" smiled Grace.

Others in the boardroom excitedly began sharing. Sig, tuning in from Canada, shared how he had consulted God about his finances, while Nasimul in Bangladesh sought divine guidance for his health. Onn, joining from Thailand, spoke of dedicating time she spends online to God. For several minutes, the virtual space resonated with testimonials from those who embraced the lesson, recounting how trusting God, expressing gratitude, and seeking divine wisdom had yielded positive results throughout their week.

Time seemed to fly as the virtual space echoed with heartfelt exclamations like "Praise the Lord," enthusiastic "Amens," and a collective "Wow, that's awesome!" The atmosphere buzzed with a shared spirit of joy and affirmation.

As the sharing gradually subsided, Rhema gushed with excitement. "These testimonies are truly wonderful! Thank you all for sharing your experiences! Grace, I sense you have another impactful lesson for us today. Is there still time?"

"Absolutely," Grace responded eagerly. On the digital whiteboard screen, she began sketching the illustration of the Belief Tree. Weaving her personal testimony into the fruit, branches, trunk, and roots, she started highlighting the choices that had shaped her and the intricate web of lies embedded in the root system.

As she shared her story, some of the faces on the screen nodded, acknowledging similar and shared experiences, while others furrowed their brows in introspection.

As she shared, however, Grace unexpectedly started feeling very self-conscious. She was bearing very deep, vulnerable areas of her life to complete strangers. This wasn't like her, so before continuing, she took a deep breath and prayed. *Lord, I'm not sure what's going on, but give me courage to continue telling my story. Sharing these concepts is easy, but being open and vulnerable in sharing my own screwups is harder than I thought! Please help me.*

Grace felt God's peace settle over her, and she felt God speak to her spirit. *It's okay, Grace. This is My will for you . . . keep going.*

Grace knew that God was calling her to trust Him in the very same ways she was teaching her audience to do. So she laid bare the lies she had once embraced about herself, God, and relationships, and all of the bad fruit it had produced in her life. As she did, she noticed Adora visibly leaning forward, hanging on to every word, while members of the church group in North Carolina exchanged knowing glances. Nasimul and Sig were nodding, seemingly in unison.

Seeing the good fruit gave Grace courage. She continued to share even her most embarrassing moments, then guided the class through the life-changing process of asking God to unearth the lies that were bearing this bad fruit. Grace explained the next steps—confessing and renouncing these lies. The more she shared, the more the participants began to understand the profound role of roots in their own Belief Trees.

Of course, if Grace was expecting the participants to share the role of roots in their Belief Trees, she knew that she had to share hers as well. Her voice trembled with the emotional weight of what she was about to do. Then she recounted the lies she, too, had once believed and how God had exchanged them for liberating truths.

Grace whispered, "When I asked God to reveal the truth He wanted me to use to replace the lie, I had a vision of my Belief Tree. As I was watching, God carved the words 'Jesus loves Grace!' on the trunk." The ripple effect of those words seemed to touch every heart.

Grace allowed for a contemplative pause, then brightened. "That's a perfect place to stop. Thank you for having me!"

Shekinah and Rhema thanked Grace for sharing. As their closing remarks were being made, Grace once again was drawn to the unnamed caller. The question lingered in her mind like a puzzle itching to be solved. Then almost in response to her unspoken question came a voice she recognized. "Grace, your lesson truly resonated with me. Can I secure a spot on your Freedom Wall as well?" Grace's heart skipped a beat. It was Dr. Max. "And if you're willing, perhaps a special place in your heart too?"

A harmonious "Oooh, Grace!" rippled through the online participants, a collective and playful response for their new friend.

THE PRESCRIPTION

Chapter 6

# THE PRESCRIPTION

*A merry heart does good, like medicine, but a broken spirit dries the bones. Proverbs 17:22*

---

Grace folded and unfolded Max's note several times, then gently tucked it back into her journal. The note would bookmark the day she brought her mom back to Dr. Miracle's office for a follow-up appointment, confirming the Type 2 Diabetes diagnosis.

She remembered the appointment well. While waiting for the doctor to appear, she once again studied the menagerie of plastic organs displayed on the counter in the exam room. At the very moment Dr. Miracle opened the exam room door, the model heart toppled off the shelf and into her hands. Max moved toward her, gazed into her wide-open eyes, leaned over, and whispered, "Grace, you're holding my heart."

Reminiscing, Grace gushed: *You're holding my heart! Who says that? It's so romantic!*

She struggled to pay attention as the handsome physician outlined her mom's essential lifestyle modifications. He suggested embracing a well-balanced diet, incorporating more physical activity into her routine, and acquiring a blood sugar monitor for effective self-monitoring.

As Grace and her mom headed out the door, the girl at the front desk handed her the doctor's note, which was scribbled on a page from his prescription pad. The words were difficult to decipher, but the message was clear.

Grinning, she sat up in her hammock to divulge Max's scribbles to the ceramic gnome next door. "He said, 'Help! ICU in my future.' Can you believe that? For heaven's sake, the guy loves the Lord, he's good looking, obviously smart, and he's got a sense of humor!"

Without warning, the old feelings of worthlessness swept through her mind and darkened her mood. *Who do I think I am? No man will ever love me. I don't deserve anyone, let alone a "Maximus Miracle."*

Realizing the old lies were trying to take root in her again, Grace went to battle by quoting the words from her dream, the words carved into the apple tree, "Jesus loves Grace." She took a shaky breath and spoke out loud. "I command the lies to leave in Jesus' name!"

Grace opened her journal and wrote down her thoughts, *My decisions regarding men used to be motivated by the fear of being rejected or my endless pursuit for acceptance. I believed lies, and those lies produced bad fruit in my life.*

Proverbs 4:23 popped into her mind. She pondered the words of this familiar verse, which she fashioned into a prayer and recorded in her journal. *I will guard my heart because it determines the direction of my life. Lord, please don't allow any man into my life unless that relationship is from You. I choose to trust You. Keep me on the path that leads to life. Help me follow what Your Spirit wants.*

Grace picked up her phone as it chimed with a text notification from "the good doctor." Although deciphering Max's handwriting proved to be like reading Egyptian hieroglyphics, his text painted a clear picture regarding his budding interest. Neighbor Gnome seemed more interested in a dandelion near his feet than Grace's love life, but she read the message aloud for his benefit. "Grace, I hope you're a cardiologist, because something is going on with my heart. Need an appointment ASAP." The message ended with a heart icon.

Grace bowed her head and continued praying. Guard my heart, Lord. She asked God how to reply, when to reply, and what to reply. When she sensed His peace, Grace typed her reply and ended it with a smiley face. "Well, I'm not a cardiologist, but I usually don't miss a beat. Does that mean you are asking me out?"

She held her breath and stared at her phone until Max replied seconds later.

"My mom taught me to listen to my heart, Grace. I'm thinking 'boom-boom, boom-boom' means let's meet for coffee Friday morning at Solomon's Bakery."

---

Early Friday morning, Grace sat quietly in her prayer chair, cross-legged and resting her head back on the cross-stitch pillow she made in eighth grade. The faded, blue lettering showcased a good reminder, "Trust in the Lord with all your heart."

Squeezing her eyes shut, Grace pictured Jesus sitting across the room in the chair in front of her. The love in His eyes brought tears to hers.

*Lord, thank You for loving me. Help me focus on Your acceptance today! I want to be who You made me to be and not strive for man's acceptance—Max's acceptance. Protect my heart. Protect his heart too! May we enjoy our time and honor You in everything we say and do. In Jesus' name. Amen!*

---

Time flew as Max and Grace chatted on and on in the red leatherette booth at Solomon's Bakery. Waiters came and went. The aroma of fresh bread baking filled the air. Coffee grew cold; pastries became hard; but the conversation was warm, uplifting, and healthy. In regular intervals, their laughter could be heard throughout the shop.

Grace marveled to herself, *Hmmm . . . a merry heart does do good, like medicine.*

# Chapter 7

# GRACE-FILLED MIRACLES

*Confess your sins to each other and pray for each other so that you may be healed. The earnest prayer of a righteous person has great power and produces wonderful results. James 5:16 (NLT)*

---

Max sat across from Grace in what had now become their favorite booth at Solomon's Bakery. It was early and the sun was just starting to rise, casting a soft glow over the table as they sipped their coffee. The aroma of cinnamon rolls made Grace's stomach growl.

Max and Grace had been seeing each other six weeks.

"Grace, there's something I've been longing to confide in you. Your lesson on decisions sparked a profound revelation in me, unraveling the motives behind many of my choices," Max confessed, his voice barely rising above a whisper.

Grace looked up from her half-eaten cinnamon roll, concern etched across her face. "What is it, Max?"

Max inhaled deeply, trying to compose himself. "We haven't talked a lot about our past relationships, but I was married."

Grace's mind suddenly flooded with questions. Was he divorced? Had he been widowed? She could feel her anxiety building. What did this mean for their relationship? She looked at Max, her eyes full of compassion and curiosity, but her heart was pounding.

"Tell me about it," Grace said gently.

It was obvious Max's heart was heavy as he spoke. He explained that they had only been married one year, but they were in love. His voice trembled with emotion as he explained further.

"Five years ago, we were traveling through Asia when we caught COVID-19. Sarah was born with a heart condition. In fact, that's how we met. She was going through testing at the hospital where I was doing my residency. Since childhood, her doctors had told her parents she wouldn't live long. But she defied their expectations and outlived predictions. Unfortunately, with her weak heart, the virus was too much for her to overcome. Had we been allowed back in the States, she might have pulled through," Max explained.

Grace's eyes widened in shock as she took in the weight of his words. She reached out and took his hand in hers, squeezing it tightly in silent support.

Max spoke about his late wife and shared fond memories of their travels together. He talked about the time they visited Paris and strolled along the Seine, watching the Eiffel Tower light up at night. He also reminisced about their love of good food and how they would try out new restaurants and dishes wherever they went. Max even shared some of their silly inside jokes, like the time they pretended to be spies while touring a museum, whispering secrets to each other as they wandered through the exhibits. Grace listened intently, captivated by the stories of their adventures and the love they had shared.

Max continued confiding in Grace, "You know, God taught me some life lessons with the loss of Sarah. Because we couldn't get back to America for treatment, I was angry, afraid, and in hyper-control mode, trying to fix everything. I found myself telling the doctors and nurses what to do, raging at God, fasting, praying, calling everyone I could think of and demanding that they help us get back to America, on and on. When Sarah died, I was devastated. *It was my job to save her*—or so

I thought. But it led to a life-changing revelation. I can't fix everything. I'm not in charge of whether someone lives or dies. I can't twist enough arms to get my way."

Grace noted the restrained anger in his tone.

"As I prayed about the bad fruit I saw in my life, God reminded me of a time in my childhood when I first started believing it was up to me to fix everyone's problems. I was eight years old when my mother got breast cancer and started treatments, surgery, and chemo. I was terrified she would die. Mom would squeeze my hand and beg, 'Help me, Maxie. Make the pain go away. You're the miracle I need.'"

Grace sighed with growing comprehension of the effects this could have on a child.

Max nodded, "Yes, I thought it was up to me to make my mom feel better and keep her from dying. The good news is that she did recover and is still cancer-free, but that lie from the enemy took root in my life. It might have even been my motivation for going to medical school and becoming a doctor. When God revealed this to me, I forgave my mom for putting such a massive burden on me. I know she didn't mean to, but I took it to heart. I repented of the lie that I had to control everything or people would die. I'd been taking God's place by not trusting His control. Sadly, I still struggle at times with that."

Grace repeated back to show she had been listening before making any suggestions. "I hear you saying the Lord reminded you of your mother's words when she was sick with cancer, and those words went deep into your heart and mind. The lie that you're the one who needs to fix everyone's problems or keep them from dying produced the bad fruit of anger, fear, control, and manipulation."

Max smiled, "Did I really say all that?"

Grace returned the smile and continued, "I might have added the manipulation part."

Max agreed, "Yes, there's been manipulation."

Grace tilted her head sweetly, "Okay. You said you've prayed and want to get rid of those negative emotions and behaviors. You've forgiven. You've repented, but you still feel stuck. Is that close?"

Max gave a nod, confirming she was on the right track.

Grace put on her counselor's hat and spoke softly, "Perhaps the piece that is missing is replacing the lie with God's truth. You don't want to leave an empty place for the enemy to come back in. Right?" Grace smiled at him. "Would you like to pray together or would you want to pray later on your own?"

Max quickly replied, "Let's pray right now."

"Great! I'd love to join you. Let's ask God to replace that lie with His truth and then be quiet to listen. You might think of a Bible verse, or He may show you something else. Jesus said in Matthew 7:11, 'If you then, being evil, know how to give good gifts to your children, how much more will your Father who is in heaven give good things to those who ask Him.' You can ask your Heavenly Father for a gift, and you can be sure He won't give you a stone or a snake."

"That's a good word, Grace. I'm ready to pray."

Max bowed his head and prayed out loud as if they were the only ones in the bakery. "Heavenly Father, I've believed the lie that it's up to me to heal people and keep them from dying. That lie has permeated my life, career, previous marriage, thoughts, and emotions. Remove that lie, Lord, and replace it with Your truth. I wait on You to speak to me." Max was gripping Grace's hand.

Grace silently prayed for the Lord to speak to Max. "What's the Lord showing you, Max?"

With his eyes still tightly shut, Max spoke, "It's like I hear God blowing."

"What does that mean to you?"

"It's the breath of life. He's the life-giver, not me. He's showing me that He breathed His life into Sarah. She's alive and perfectly healed. I see her talking to Jesus and then throwing her head back and laughing like we used to do." Tears flowed. Lies were replaced with an encounter with God.

---

In the following weeks, Max and Grace found themselves spending an increasing amount of time together. They extended their companionship to include Grace's mom on leisurely walks, creating a cozy trio. The joy of preparing nutritious meals and healthy desserts became a shared pastime, filling their moments with warmth and laughter.

A few months later, during a festive Christmas shopping spree, surrounded by the array of perfumes at the cologne counter, Max drew her wrist close to his nose, savoring the new fragrance she had just tried. As he lovingly embraced her entire arm, the warmth and intimacy of his touch sent a shiver through her, making her heart race. As she studied his closed eyes and enraptured face, Grace realized the depth of his affection.

*Lord, I think this man loves me! You healed me of the lie that I was unlovable and undesirable. Your love freed me from chasing men for acceptance and approval. Now, by some miracle, You brought Max into my life. Please guide our future. Thank You!*

Perhaps as lost in silent prayer as she was, Max finally opened his eyes and gazed deeply through the windows of her soul. He gently kissed her hand and then dropped to one knee. His voice steady but filled with emotion, he said, "Grace, remember when I said, 'You hold my heart'? Those weren't just words. Since I met you, my broken heart has healed. It beats again. I love you more than words can express. Will you marry me?" As he spoke, he raised his other hand to reveal a dazzling engagement ring, its brilliance outshone only by the astonished joy in Grace's eyes.

Grace beamed at him. "As you know, I never thought any man would or could love me. But it looks like God has worked a miracle and brought healing into both of our hearts. Marry you? My answer is yes!"

The store assistants witnessed a love story unfold amidst the perfume bottles, their own hearts warmed by the romance and the sweet fragrance of Christmas cheer that filled the air.

# CONCLUSION

You've just completed Grace's story, and now it's time to embark on your own journey. You've learned the importance of making decisions based on the guidance of the Spirit rather than the desires of the flesh. As you move forward, we encourage you to apply these lessons to your life.

Remember, you have been given the gift of freedom to produce good fruit by aligning your decisions with God's will. Though it may not always be easy, and you will face temptations and struggles, continue to trust in God and lean on Him.

The 21-Day Challenge for Change is a powerful tool to help you make better decisions and replace lies with truth. Approach each day with intention, allowing the Spirit to lead you. As the truth sets you free, you will grow and transform.

As Galatians 5:17–19 reminds us, there's a battle between our flesh and the Spirit. By choosing to follow the Spirit, we produce good fruit in our lives. Keep this book close, refer to it whenever you need guidance, and share what you've learned with others who are seeking direction and want to produce good fruit.

Like God said, "Choose life and blessings!"

# 21-DAY CHALLENGE FOR CHANGE

Days 1 – 5
MAKING GOOD DECISIONS

Days 6 – 11
PRODUCING GOOD FRUIT

Days 12 – 16
5 TRUTHS ABOUT GOD

Days 17 – 21
DEVOTIONAL PRAYERS

# Days 1 – 5

# MAKING GOOD DECISIONS

*Avoiding Decisions Motivated by the Flesh*

---

As we journey through life, we often face crossroads that challenge our faith and decision-making. In these moments, it's crucial to remember the importance of following God's path rather than relying on our own understanding. The Bible provides us with timeless wisdom and guidance to navigate these challenges.

For the next five days, we will embark on a transformative journey, starting with evaluating your past decisions using the Decision Diagram from Chapter 4. As the days progress, you'll learn how to make better decisions rooted in trusting God, thanking God, and asking God. This journey will help you reflect on moments when you chose your own path over God's and faced negative consequences, empowering you to realign with His plan and experience the abundant life He promises.

HEALING GRACE: Practical Steps to Producing Good Fruit by Replacing Lies with Truth

# Day 1
# Evaluating Your Past Decision-Making

*"There is a path before each person that seems right, but it ends in death." Proverbs 14:12 (NLT)*

We continually are making decisions in various areas of life: spiritual, psychological, social, physical, financial, marital, and parental. If we neglect to seek divine guidance—whether due to forgetfulness, refusal, or lack of awareness—we inevitably default to following our fleshly inclinations.

*"For the mind set on the flesh is death, but the mind set on the Spirit is life and peace." Romans 8:6 (NASB)*

Contemplate the significance of your choices. Choosing to follow God's guidance leads to life—joy and peace. Conversely, following selfish desires, or "the flesh," leads to frustration and loss.

Reflect on any area of life where you might be experiencing "death" due to wrong choices. Write down what comes to your mind.

_____

_____

_____

What motivations, such as selfishness, pride, vanity, defending your rights, or fear, influenced those decisions? If you don't know, ask God. Write down what He shows you.

_____

_____

_____

Days 1–5 MAKING GOOD DECISIONS

Read Proverbs 14:12. Did your decision seem "right" to you at the time? Explain how you justified it.

_____
_____
_____

Are you ready to change directions and go God's way? You can either write a prayer of confession, asking God to remind you to seek His guidance in your decisions, or use the following prayer.

*Heavenly Father, I come before You with a humble heart, acknowledging the times I've made decisions motivated by the flesh—driven by selfishness, pride, vanity, defending my rights, or fear. I repent for choosing my own way instead of seeking Your guidance and wisdom. Forgive me for the mistakes and negative consequences that have resulted from these choices.*

*Lord, I ask for Your forgiveness and for the strength to turn away from these motivations. Give me wisdom and discernment as I move forward, so that my decisions may reflect Your will and bring about positive outcomes.*

*Thank You for Your forgiveness. Guide me in making choices that honor You and bring forth good fruit in my life. In Jesus' name, I pray, Amen.*

_____
_____
_____
_____
_____

# Day 2
# Decide to Choose Life

*"Today I have given you the choice between life and death, between blessings and curses. Now I call on heaven and earth to witness the choice you make. Oh, that you would choose life, so that you and your descendants might live." Deuteronomy 30:19 (NLT)*

Think of a specific decision you need to make in one area of life. (Some issues will affect multiple areas.) What decision do you need to make? What area(s) of life are involved?

___

___

___

*"The Lord says, 'I will guide you along the best pathway for your life. I will advise you and watch over you.'" Psalm 32:8 (NLT)*

How does this verse shape your approach to making decisions?

___

___

___

God's guidance is available to you whenever you seek it. Remain open to His direction and trust that He knows the best path for your life.

Days 1 – 5 MAKING GOOD DECISIONS

Based on the Decision Diagram, how is God guiding you to follow the Spirit in your decision? Is He prompting you to trust, thank, or ask Him?

_____

_____

_____

*"Your word is a lamp to guide my feet and a light for my path."*
*Psalm 119:105 (NLT)*

If you feel uncertain about your ability to hear from God, remember that the Bible is our guide and will illuminate the way. Ask God to speak to you through His Word and then take time to read it.

Do you feel pulled toward making your decision after the flesh (selfishness, pride, vanity, defending your rights, or fear)? Explain.

_____

_____

_____

That's the battle we are in–the Spirit verses the Flesh. We decide which one we will surrender to.

*Heavenly Father, thank You for Your promise to guide and watch over me. Help me to hear Your voice clearly and to follow the path You have set before me. Give me the wisdom to discern Your will and the courage to choose Your way over my fleshly desires. Strengthen me to overcome selfishness, pride, and fear, and to walk in obedience to You. In Jesus' name, Amen.*

# Day 3
# Trusting God to Meet Your Needs

*"And my God shall supply all your need according to His riches in glory by Christ Jesus." Philippians 4:19*

God desires for you to trust Him when you face needs in your life. However, in the midst of a need, it's common to forget how capable God is of meeting those needs. Trusting God means learning to wait on Him, confident in His ability to provide.

When it comes to trusting God, several factors might be at play. Take a moment to reflect on whether any of the following questions resonate with your experience. Read the verses and choose to believe what God says instead of how you feel or what you have thought in the past.

Do doubts about God's goodness undermine your trust in Him? What does Psalm 34:8 clarify for you? Write your thoughts.

*"Oh, taste and see that the Lord is good; Blessed is the man who trusts in Him!" Psalm 34:8*

Do past disappointments or unanswered prayers affect your ability to trust God? What does Galatians 6:9 teach you about persevering through these challenges?

*"And let us not grow weary while doing good, for in due season we shall reap if we do not lose heart." Galatians 6:9*

Days 1 – 5 MAKING GOOD DECISIONS

Are you finding it hard to trust God because you want to control your own life and outcomes? What does Proverbs 3:7 reveal about how you should approach this challenge?

*"Do not be wise in your own eyes; Fear the Lord and depart from evil." Proverbs 3:7*

Are you relying on your own abilities and wisdom instead of acknowledging your need for God's guidance? What does Proverbs 16:18 reveal about the impact of pride on your trust in the Lord?

*"Pride goes before destruction, And a haughty spirit before a fall." Proverbs 16:18*

Do you struggle to believe that you can hear from God? How does John 10:27 reassure you of your ability to hear His voice?

*"My sheep hear My voice, and I know them, and they follow Me." John 10:27*

*Heavenly Father, thank You for Your promise to guide and provide for me. As I face doubts and fears that challenge my trust in You, I ask for Your help to overcome these obstacles. Grant me the humility to acknowledge my need for Your guidance and the courage to rely on Your wisdom rather than my own.*

*Help me to let go of my need to control outcomes. Strengthen my faith and remind me of Your goodness and faithfulness. May I trust You fully, even in the midst of uncertainty, and find peace in Your loving presence. In Jesus' name. Amen.*

# Day 4
# Thanking God for All Things

*"In everything give thanks; for this is the will of God in Christ Jesus for you." 1 Thessalonians 5:18*

When life is going well, what should you do? Express your gratitude to God by thanking Him. And when you are experiencing problems or difficulties? Your response should be the same: thank Him. When you thank God for all things, your faith grows, you reaffirm your trust in His faithfulness, and a profound sense of gladness and joy begins to well up within you.

The opposite is true when we refuse to thank God—we experience doubts, fear, and depression. Many people link their depression to their problems. However, the truth is that everyone faces challenges, yet not everyone feels depressed. Romans 1:21 sheds light on a potential cause of a dark and confused mind, which can often resemble depression.

*"Yes, they knew God, but they wouldn't worship Him as God or even give Him thanks. And they began to think up foolish ideas of what God was like. As a result, their minds became dark and confused." Romans 1:21 (NLT)*

That verse points out that failing to worship God and give Him thanks can lead to negative mental and emotional conditions. Gaining a positive mental attitude may be as simple as thanking God for all things.

As Ephesians 5:20 encourages, let us give thanks always for all things.

*"Giving thanks always for all things to God the Father in the name of our Lord Jesus Christ." Ephesians 5:20*

Days 1 – 5 MAKING GOOD DECISIONS

What is a problem you're experiencing that you need to thank God for today?

_____
_____
_____

Write a prayer of praise, expressing your gratitude for this situation.

_____
_____
_____

How can shifting your focus from your problems to God change your perspective on the difficulties you face?

_____
_____
_____

How can regularly practicing gratitude toward God influence your mental and emotional well-being?

_____
_____
_____

As we conclude this reflection on the power of gratitude, let us come before God in prayer, thanking Him for His guidance and love, and asking Him to help us embrace His presence in every moment of our lives.

*Heavenly Father, I come before You with a heart full of gratitude. Thank You for Your unwavering love and faithfulness. I acknowledge both the blessings and the challenges in my life, trusting that You are working all things together for good. Even in the midst of difficulties, I know You are shaping me to be more like Jesus.*

*Thank You for the good times that bring joy and for the trials that teach me to rely on You. Your hand is evident in every circumstance, guiding me, molding me, and drawing me closer to the image of Your Son. Help me to love like Jesus, to forgive as He forgave, and to obey as He did.*

*Thank You for Your constant presence and for the promise that You are making all things new. In Jesus' name, Amen.*

Days 1 – 5 MAKING GOOD DECISIONS

# Day 5
# Asking God for Wisdom

*"If you need wisdom, ask our generous God, and He will give it to you. He will not rebuke you for asking." James 1:5 (NLT)*

Trust God with your needs, thank Him for your problems, and when you have questions, ask Him. How do you make decisions when you don't know what to do? Sometimes the lack of clarity comes simply because we haven't asked God for guidance.

The world, the flesh, and the devil want to prevent you from asking God for direction and wisdom, leading you to believe that God is not interested in your life.

The Lie: "God doesn't care about your questions, decisions, or problems."

The Truth is found in James 1:5.

What questions do you have today? Write them down and then spend time talking to God about them.

_____

_____

_____

_____

Satan wants to keep you in confusion and doubt.

The Lie: "You don't need God's guidance; you can figure it out on your own."

The Truth is found in Proverbs 3:5–6.

> *"Trust in the Lord with all your heart, and lean not on your own understanding; in all your ways acknowledge Him, and He shall direct your paths."* Proverbs 3:5–6

Where can you start to trust God more and rely less on your own understanding in your decision-making process?

_____

_____

By recognizing these lies and focusing on God's promises, you can make decisions with confidence and trust in His guidance.

Here's a powerful reminder of God's promise to speak to you and give you guidance:

> *"Your ears shall hear a word behind you, saying, 'This is the way, walk in it,' whenever you turn to the right hand or whenever you turn to the left."* Isaiah 30:21

How can you create space in your daily life to listen for God's guidance and follow His direction?

_____

_____

As we close this section of the 21-Day Challenge for Change, let's pray.

> *Heavenly Father, remind me to come to You and ask for Your wisdom and direction. I acknowledge that sometimes I forget. Your plan is the best plan. Your way is the best way.*
>
> *I thank You for Your countless blessings and for the challenges that come my way. In every circumstance, I choose to lift my voice in thanksgiving, knowing that You are always with me. Help me to see Your hand at work in every situation and to remain steadfast in my faith.*

Days 1 – 5 MAKING GOOD DECISIONS

*Thank You, Lord, for Your unfailing love and for the assurance that You are always in control. I surrender my worries, fears, and doubts to You, and I praise You for the victory that is already mine in Christ Jesus. In Jesus' name, I pray, Amen.*

# Days 6 – 11

# PRODUCING GOOD FRUIT

*Replacing Lies with Truth*

In our story, we use the analogy of a tree producing good or bad fruit. Each part of the tree represents different aspects of our life. The roots symbolize our belief system—whether we are believing truth or lies. The trunk represents our core values and wants, such as being loved, accepted, significant, or safe. The branches signify the decisions we make to satisfy those values and needs. The fruit represents the outcome of our decisions—our actions, emotions, attitudes, and relationships, whether good or bad.

For the next six days, you will focus on the Belief Tree lesson, which we explained in Chapter 2.

HEALING GRACE: Practical Steps to Producing Good Fruit by Replacing Lies with Truth

# Day 6
# Fruit: Identifying Your Fruit

*"Now the deeds of the flesh are evident, which are: sexual immorality, impurity, indecent behavior, idolatry, witchcraft, hostilities, strife, jealousy, outbursts of anger, selfish ambition, dissensions, factions, envy, drunkenness, carousing, and things like these." Galatians 5:19–21 (NASB)*

Reflect on the deeds of the flesh listed in Galatians 5:19–21. What bad fruit do you see in your life, actions, emotions, attitudes, and relationships? Write these down.

_____

_____

Most Christians are bothered when they see bad fruit in their lives. So they try to remove it, but it often just grows back.

*"People who conceal their sins will not prosper, but if they confess and turn from them, they will receive mercy."*
*Proverbs 28:13 (NLT)*

What have you done to try to remove or hide the bad fruit in your life?

_____

_____

Reflecting on the bad fruit in our lives and understanding that true change comes from God, let's bring our struggles to Him in prayer:

## Days 6 – 11 PRODUCING GOOD FRUIT

*Heavenly Father, I come before You, acknowledging the bad fruit that I have seen in my life. I confess that I have often tried to remove or hide it on my own, only to see it return. I realize now that true transformation comes from You alone.*

*Lord, I ask for Your mercy and guidance. Help me to identify the root causes of this bad fruit and to bring them to light. I confess my sins to You and turn away from them, trusting in Your promise of forgiveness.*

*Give me the strength and wisdom to address these issues at their roots, to replace lies with Your truth, and to make decisions that align with Your will. Help me to rely on Your Spirit to produce good fruit in my life.*

*Thank You, Father, for Your unfailing love and Your healing grace. I surrender my struggles to You and ask for Your help in becoming more like Christ each day. In Jesus' name, I pray, Amen.*

*Surrender your life to God. When the Holy Spirit guides your decisions, the fruit of your life will be good.*

*"But the Holy Spirit produces this kind of fruit in our lives: love, joy, peace, patience, kindness, goodness, faithfulness, gentleness, and self-control." Galatians 5:22–23 (NLT)*

# Day 7
# Branches: Evaluating Your Decisions

*"You will always harvest what you plant. Those who live only to satisfy their own sinful nature will harvest decay and death from that sinful nature. But those who live to please the Spirit will harvest everlasting life from the Spirit." Galatians 6:7–8 (NLT)*

Fruit doesn't just appear on a tree; it grows on the branches. The branches represent your decisions. What our lives produce will be a direct result of the decisions we make. The fruit symbolizes the consequences of these choices– good or bad fruit.

Reflect on the decisions you've made in the past and the fruit they have produced. Consider the Decision Diagram in chapter 4.

What motivations, such as selfishness, pride, vanity, defending your rights, or fear, influenced your decisions?

_____
_____
_____

How have your choices contributed to the outcomes you're experiencing? Write down what comes to mind.

_____
_____
_____

God presents us with choices that lead to either life and blessings or death and curses. The decisions we make determine the fruit we bear.

## Days 6 – 11 PRODUCING GOOD FRUIT

*"Today I have given you the choice between life and death, between blessings and curses. Now I call on heaven and earth to witness the choice you make. Oh, that you would choose life, so that you and your descendants might live!" Deuteronomy 30:19 (NLT)*

How can you ensure that your daily decisions align with choosing life and blessings, resulting in good fruit in your life and the lives of those around you?

_____
_____

Following the humility and selflessness of Christ in our decisions ensures that our choices produce good fruit and reflect His character.

*"You must have the same attitude that Christ Jesus had. Though he was God, He did not think of equality with God as something to cling to. Instead, He gave up His divine privileges; He took the humble position of a slave and was born as a human being." Philippians 2:5–7 (NLT)*

How can adopting the attitude of Christ in your decisions lead to better outcomes and fruit that glorifies God?

_____
_____

Trusting in the Lord and placing our hope in Him leads to stability and continual fruitfulness, regardless of external circumstances.

*"But blessed are those who trust in the Lord and have made the Lord their hope and confidence. They are like trees planted along a riverbank, with roots that reach deep into the water. Such trees are not bothered by the heat or worried by long months of drought. Their leaves stay green, and they never stop producing fruit." Jeremiah 17:7–8 (NLT)*

# HEALING GRACE: Practical Steps to Producing Good Fruit by Replacing Lies with Truth

Ask God to show you how to deepen your trust in Him so that your decisions, like branches on a tree, consistently produce good fruit. Write down what He reveals to you.

_____
_____
_____
_____
_____
_____

As we reflect on the importance of our decisions and their impact on our lives, let us commit to making choices that align with God's will and produce good fruit. By trusting in Him and allowing the Holy Spirit to guide us, we can ensure that our lives reflect His love and grace.

*Heavenly Father, I come before You, acknowledging that every decision I make shapes the course of my life. I surrender my will to You, trusting that You will guide me in the right path. Fill me with Your Holy Spirit, so that my choices reflect Your love, wisdom, and goodness. Help me to seek Your guidance in every situation and to listen to Your voice with a willing and obedient heart. May my life bear the fruit of righteousness, bringing glory to Your name. Thank You for Your unfailing love and for always being with me. In Jesus' name, I pray. Amen.*

Days 6 – 11 PRODUCING GOOD FRUIT

# Day 8
# Trunk: Exploring Your Core Values

*"Yet you don't have what you want because you don't ask God for it. And even when you ask, you don't get it because your motives are all wrong—you want only what will give you pleasure."*
*James 4:2-3 (NLT)*

The branches of a tree are attached to the trunk, which represents our core values, wants, or needs. These values might include desires to be loved, accepted, significant, or safe. Our values, shaped by what we may have lacked, deeply influence our decisions.

What motivates your decisions? Why did you choose to act the way you did? While your values or wants may not be inherently evil, the methods you choose to satisfy them can be. God created us with needs, and only He can truly fulfill them. When we doubt His provision, we often try to meet these needs ourselves.

Identify your core values or desires. What do you deeply want or value? (For example: to be loved, accepted, feel significant, or safe.)

_____

_____

_____

Ask God to show you when and why these needs have gone unmet.

_____

_____

_____

What actions have you taken to fulfill these desires?

_____

_____

When we seek fulfillment from others or ourselves, we often make poor choices that yield negative consequences. For instance, a desire for acceptance might lead to an immoral relationship, resulting in shame, deceit, and broken relationships.

How have these actions impacted the fruit your life is producing?

_____

_____

Jeremiah 17:5–6 states, *"Cursed is the man who trusts in man and makes flesh his strength, whose heart departs from the Lord. For he shall be like a shrub in the desert, and shall not see when good comes, but shall inhabit the parched places in the wilderness."*

God has a better plan! Instead of relying on people or things to fulfill your needs, wants, or values, shift your focus to developing a deeper relationship with Jesus. He alone can truly satisfy your desires for love, acceptance, significance, and safety.

> *"Delight yourself in the Lord; And He will give you the desires of your heart."* Psalm 37:4 (NASB)

How can you actively delight in the Lord and trust Him to fulfill the deepest desires of your heart?

_____

_____

Days 6 – 11 PRODUCING GOOD FRUIT

When we look to God to satisfy our values and desires, we make decisions that produce good fruit and lead to a fulfilling, abundant life.

*Heavenly Father, I recognize that my values and desires deeply influence my decisions. Help me to trust You to meet my needs and to seek Your guidance in every choice I make. Show me where I have tried to fulfill my desires apart from You, and help me to surrender those areas to Your loving care. May my life be rooted in Your truth, producing good fruit that glorifies You. Thank You for Your faithfulness and provision. In Jesus' name, I pray. Amen.*

# Day 9
# Roots: Recognizing Lies About Yourself

*"Let your roots grow down into Him, and let your lives be built on Him. Then your faith will grow strong in the truth you were taught, and you will overflow with thankfulness."*
*Colossians 2:7 (NLT)*

In the analogy of the tree, the roots symbolize our core beliefs—what we believe about ourselves, others, and God. Our roots draw from either truth or lies. Truth comes from God. Believing in His truth leads to vibrant, fulfilling growth and good fruit. However, lies come from the influence of Satan and the world.

As John 8:44 (NLT) reminds us, *"[Satan] has always hated the truth because there is no truth in him. When he lies, it is consistent with his character; for he is a liar and the father of lies."*

When we believe lies, it brings dysfunction and decay into our lives. False beliefs produces bad fruit.

Romans 1:28–29 (NLT) highlights the consequences of rejecting the truth: *"Since they thought it foolish to acknowledge God, He abandoned them to their foolish thinking and let them do things that should never be done. Their lives became full of every kind of wickedness, sin, greed, hate, envy, murder, quarreling, deception, malicious behavior, and gossip."*

Roots don't determine our values, but they often shape how we seek to satisfy our needs and values. For example, if you experienced an abusive or loveless childhood, it might plant a lie in you like "I'm unlovable" or "I'm worthless." Believing (the roots) that lie can cause an unhealthy attempt to fill your real need (the trunk) for love and lead to poor decisions (the branches) and ultimately bad fruit in your life.

Lies can also take root in your life from the labels you've been given or names you've been called based on your personality, abilities, looks, social standing, or behaviors—like perfectionist, stupid, plump, troublemaker, jock, promiscuous, liar, or addict. The damaging effect of lies can seep into every aspect of your life. They need to be removed and replaced with God's truth.

Ask God to reveal the lies you have knowingly or unknowingly believed regarding who you are and your worth. Write down what He shows you.

_____

_____

_____

Depending on what God reveals to you, confess the lies you've believed about yourself and repent for the ways you've tried to meet your needs apart from God, leading to poor decisions.

*Heavenly Father, I come before You humbly, acknowledging the lies I have believed about myself and the ways I have tried to meet my needs apart from You. I confess these false beliefs and the poor decisions they have led me to make. I repent for relying on my own understanding and seeking fulfillment in places that only bring harm.*

*Lord, I ask for Your forgiveness and Your help to replace these lies with Your truth. Show me how to deeply root my identity in You, knowing that I am valued, loved, and accepted by You. May Your Holy Spirit empower me to live a life that reflects Your glory and brings forth good fruit. In Jesus' name, I pray. Amen.*

Spend some time in silence, asking God to reveal His truth to you. This truth may come in various forms, such as a Bible verse that speaks directly to the lie you've believed, a worship song that reinforces God's love and promises, a vision or picture offering a new perspective through God's eyes, or a clear message or impression from the Holy Spirit. As you sit quietly, listen attentively for God's response. Be patient and allow

HEALING GRACE: Practical Steps to Producing Good Fruit by Replacing Lies with Truth

yourself to be still in His presence. When you sense God speaking to you, take note of what you hear, see, or feel, and record it here.

_____

_____

_____

*Thank You, Lord, for revealing Your truth to me. I am grateful for Your love and for showing me who I am in You. Renew my mind with this truth and let it shape my thoughts, decisions, and actions. I trust in Your Word and Your promises. In Jesus' name, Amen.*

Instead of relying on people or things to fulfill your needs, wants, or values, shift your focus to developing a deeper relationship with Jesus. He alone can truly satisfy your desires for love, acceptance, significance, and safety.

Days 6 – 11 PRODUCING GOOD FRUIT

# Day 10
# Roots: Recognizing Lies About Others

*"If someone says, 'I love God,' but hates a fellow believer, that person is a liar; for if we don't love people we can see, how can we love God, whom we cannot see?" 1 John 4:20 (NLT)*

God loves and values every person deeply. His desire is for us to reflect this love by treating others with respect, kindness, and compassion. He also calls us to pray for others, trusting that His plans for their lives will come to fruition. However, lies about others can distort our perception and interactions. These lies might include beliefs that others are inferior, have ill intentions toward us, or will never change.

Ask God to reveal the lies you have believed about others. Write down what He shows you.

_____

_____

_____

How have these lies influenced your behavior or decisions regarding others?

_____

_____

_____

When did these beliefs begin to take root in your heart and mind?

_____

_____

HEALING GRACE: Practical Steps to Producing Good Fruit by Replacing Lies with Truth

Sit silently and ask God to reveal His truth about the people you have struggled with or harbored wrong beliefs about. Spend some time in silence, asking God to reveal His truth to you.

This truth may come in various forms, such as a Bible verse that speaks directly to the lie you've believed, a worship song that reinforces God's love and promises, a vision or picture offering a new perspective through God's eyes, or a clear message or impression from the Holy Spirit.

As you sit quietly, listen attentively for God's response. Be patient and allow yourself to be still in His presence. When you sense God speaking to you, take note of what you hear, see, or feel, and record it here.

_____

_____

_____

_____

_____

*Heavenly Father, I come before You with a heart seeking Your truth and healing. Thank You for Your unconditional love for every person and for the value You place on each life. I acknowledge that I have sometimes harbored judgments and wrong beliefs about others, whether thinking they are inferior, untrustworthy, or incapable of change.*

*Lord, help me to see others through Your eyes, recognizing their worth and Your purpose in their lives. Teach me to love others as You love me, without reservation or prejudice. I choose to forgive and to pray for those who may have wronged me, trusting in Your ability to work in their lives and in mine.*

*Thank You for removing the lies I've believed about others and for healing my heart. In Jesus' name, I pray. Amen.*

Days 6 – 11 PRODUCING GOOD FRUIT

# Day 11
# Roots: Recognizing Lies About God

"God is not a man, so He does not lie. He is not human, so He does not change his mind. Has He ever spoken and failed to act? Has He ever promised and not carried it through?" Numbers 23:19 (NLT)

While God's true nature is that He is good, caring, desiring a close relationship with you, and loving you unconditionally, you may find that you have believed lies about His character. These misconceptions may stem from personal experiences or misunderstandings, but remember that our experiences do not alter the unchanging nature of God.

*"They began to think up foolish ideas of what God was like..."*
*Romans 1:21 (NLT)*

Ask God to reveal any lies you might believe about His character. Record what He shows you.

_____

_____

_____

*"See how very much our Father loves us, for he calls us His children, and that is what we are!" 1 John 3:1 (NLT)*

*"If you then, being evil, know how to give good gifts to your children, how much more will your Father who is in heaven give good things to those who ask Him!" Matthew 7:11*

How do your beliefs about God conflict with what Scripture says about Him?

_____

_____

*Heavenly Father, I come before You seeking to understand Your true nature. I confess and seek Your forgiveness for believing lies about You based on my experiences or misunderstandings. Help me to see You as You truly are—good, loving, and caring. Reveal to me any false beliefs I hold about You and replace them with Your truth. Teach me to trust in Your unchanging character and to grow in my relationship with You. Thank You for Your patience and for the grace to know You more fully. In Jesus' name, Amen.*

Sit quietly and ask God to reveal His truth about any wrong beliefs you may have held about Him. Spend some time in silence, asking God to reveal His truth to you.

This truth may come in various forms, such as a Bible verse that speaks directly to the lie you've believed, a worship song that reinforces God's love and promises, a vision or picture offering a new perspective through God's eyes, or a clear message or impression from the Holy Spirit.

As you sit quietly, listen attentively for God's response. Be patient and allow yourself to be still in His presence. When you sense God speaking to you, take note of what you hear, see, or feel, and record it here.

_____

_____

_____

_____

_____

Reflect upon and renew your mind with the truths God has shown you over the past six days—truths about yourself, others, and Him.

## Days 6 – 11 PRODUCING GOOD FRUIT

Consider how believing and internalizing these truths can transform your perspective and lead to producing good fruit in your life.

Remember, transformation and producing good fruit will happen as you focus on God's truth. Draw from Him the love, acceptance, significance, or safety you long for in your life (the trunk of the tree).

In this section of the 21-Day Challenge for Change, we've journeyed from examining the fruit to delving into the roots. God has revealed the lies that have shaped our values, decisions, and experiences. We've confronted misconceptions about ourselves, others, and God and observed how these false beliefs affect the outcomes in our lives.

By identifying and addressing these distortions, we can now replace them with God's enduring truth. As we move forward to explore the Five Truths about God, hold on to your new insights, which will renew your mind.

# Days 12 – 16

# 5 TRUTHS ABOUT GOD

It's crucial to grasp the Five Fundamental Truths about God. Why? Because if our understanding of God is skewed, it will undermine our trust in Him, our ability to be thankful, and our willingness to ask for His guidance or help.

God is much more than these five truths, of course, but without understanding these foundational truths—that He exists, that He is all-powerful, that He is good, that He loves you, and that He keeps His promises—it's like having a blurry picture of Him. We might end up trying to take on His role ourselves or fill the void with something else.

Getting to know who God truly is becomes a game-changer in how we navigate life and connect with Him.

# Day 12
# TRUTH #1: Believe in God's Existence

*"And it is impossible to please God without faith. Anyone who wants to come to Him must believe that God exists and that He rewards those who sincerely seek Him." Hebrews 11:6 (NLT)*

The foundation of our faith begins with this fundamental truth: believing in God's existence. Hebrews 11:6 highlights the importance of faith and trust in the reality of God. Reflecting on what it means to believe in God's existence is crucial for deepening our relationship with Him and experiencing His presence in our lives.

How does knowing that you need faith to please God affect how you approach your relationship with Him and your trust in His promises?

_____

_____

_____

Many people resist the idea of believing in God, desiring independence and control over their own lives. However, this resistance often leads to negative consequences and bondage, producing bad fruit, such as confusion, false beliefs, addictions, and inner turmoil, which ultimately strips them of true freedom and fulfillment.

*"Only fools say in their hearts, 'There is no God.' They are corrupt, and their actions are evil; not one of them does good." Psalm 14:1 (NLT)*

Relying solely on our own understanding can make us foolish, believing we're wise enough to navigate our lives on our own.

*"Trust in the Lord with all your heart and lean not on your own understanding; in all your ways acknowledge Him, and He shall direct your paths." Proverbs 3:5–6*

How does Proverbs 3:5–6 encourage you to trust in God's guidance and submit to His authority in your life despite the desire for personal control?

___

___

___

The presence of suffering, pain, and evil in the world often leads people to question the existence of God. They struggle to reconcile a loving God with the harsh realities of life. However, suffering is a result of sin and the fall of Adam, and not something God causes. We choose life or death. God wants us to choose life.

> *"People ruin their lives by their own foolishness and then are angry at the Lord." Proverbs 19:3 (NLT)*

Regardless of whether our pain stems from living in a fallen world, the consequences of our own choices, or the actions of others, we can be assured that God is working through it all for our ultimate good. As Romans 8:18 reminds us, the difficulties we face now are nothing compared to the glory that will be revealed in us.

> *"For I consider that the sufferings of this present time are not worthy to be compared with the glory which shall be revealed in us." Romans 8:18*

Considering Romans 8:18, how can you find hope and perspective in your own suffering, knowing that it is not comparable to the future glory promised by God?

___

___

___

HEALING GRACE: Practical Steps to Producing Good Fruit by Replacing Lies with Truth

What are some ways you can strengthen your faith in God's existence?

_____
_____
_____
_____
_____

As we reflect on the importance of believing in God's existence, let us ask Him to strengthen our faith and help us overcome any doubts that may be holding us back.

*Heavenly Father, I come before You acknowledging the need for faith to truly understand and embrace Your presence in my life. Help me to believe wholeheartedly in Your existence and to trust in Your promises, even when I face doubts or challenges.*

*Strengthen my faith and open my heart to the reality of Your presence, so I can fully experience the guidance and comfort You provide. Teach me to trust in Your ways and seek Your wisdom in every aspect of my life. I pray that through Your grace, I may overcome any resistance and embrace the assurance that You are real and actively working for my good. I want to express my gratitude for making Yourself known to me. I surrender every area of my life to You. In Jesus' name, amen.*

# Day 13
# TRUTH #2: Believe God is All-Powerful

*"Look, God is all-powerful. Who is a teacher like Him?"*
*Job 36:22 (NLT)*

The second essential truth you need to believe about God is not only that He exists, but that He is all-powerful. He knows everything, is everywhere, and is in complete command and control.

The world, your own flesh, and the devil might try to convince you that God is not all-powerful to undermine your trust in His strength and control.

Here's the truth to counter the lies that try to undermine your faith:

*"Let your roots grow down into Him, and let your lives be built on Him. Then your faith will grow strong in the truth you were taught, and you will overflow with thankfulness." Colossians 2:7 (NLT)*

How does building your life on God through prayer, Bible reading, and involvement in a Christian community help strengthen your faith in His power?

_____

_____

_____

Here's the truth to counter the lies that try to foster fear and anxiety:

*"Fear not, for I am with you; Be not dismayed, for I am your God. I will strengthen you, Yes, I will help you, I will uphold you with My righteous right hand." Isaiah 41:10*

How can trusting in God's promise to strengthen and uphold you help alleviate your fears and anxieties?

_____

_____

_____

In what ways can you acknowledge God's all-powerful nature in your life?

_____

_____

_____

How does understanding God's omnipotence affect your trust in Him during challenging times?

_____

_____

_____

Here's the truth to counter the lies that try to promote self-reliance:

*"Some trust in chariots, and some in horses, but we will remember the name of the Lord our God." Psalm 20:7*

In what areas of your life do you need to stop relying on your own understanding or other things and start trusting in God?

_____

_____

_____

## Days 12 – 16  5 TRUTHS ABOUT GOD

As we reflect on the importance of believing God is all-powerful, let us ask Him to strengthen our faith and help us overcome any lies that may be holding us back.

*Heavenly Father, I come before You acknowledging Your supreme power and control over all things. Help me to fully recognize and submit to Your authority in my life. Teach me to trust You completely, knowing that Your power is unmatched and that You are always in control.*

*Strengthen my faith to believe in Your ability to handle every situation. Help me resist and reject any lies that undermine my faith, foster fear and anxiety, or promote self-dependence. Instead, let me rest in Your truth and rely on Your all-encompassing strength. In Jesus' name, Amen.*

# Day 14
# TRUTH #3: Believe in God's Goodness

*"The Lord is good, a strong refuge when trouble comes. He is close to those who trust in him." Nahum 1:7 (NLT)*

The third foundational truth about God is that, beyond His existence and omnipotence, He is good. God is overflowing with compassion, kindness, and mercy.

Understanding that God is good in every aspect of His character is crucial to our faith. It means believing that His intentions toward us are always filled with benevolence, even when we don't fully understand His ways. This truth not only deepens our relationship with Him but also strengthens our trust, knowing that His goodness guides His actions and decisions in our lives.

Satan wants to make us question God's inherent goodness, leading us to doubt His intentions and care for us.

*"Whatever is good and perfect is a gift coming down to us from God our Father, who created all the lights in the heavens. He never changes or casts a shifting shadow." James 1:17 (NLT)*

How does understanding that every good and perfect gift, not things that are evil or subpar, comes from God influence your perspective on His goodness and His role in your life?

_____

_____

_____

Days 12 – 16 5 TRUTHS ABOUT GOD

How have you experienced God's goodness in your life, especially during difficult times?

_____

_____

_____

By casting doubt on God's goodness, Satan encourages us to rely on our own abilities and wisdom rather than trusting in God's provision and care.

*"If you then, being evil, know how to give good gifts to your children, how much more will your Father who is in heaven give good things to those who ask Him!" Matthew 7:11*

How does this verse help you understand the depth of God's goodness and His willingness to give good gifts to those who ask Him?

_____

_____

_____

As we consider the truth of God's goodness, let us seek His guidance to deepen our faith and overcome any doubts or misconceptions that might be hindering our trust in His goodness.

*Heavenly Father, thank You for the reminder of Your goodness and the perfect gifts You give us. I ask You to strengthen my faith in Your unfailing goodness, especially in times of doubt or difficulty. Help me to recognize and trust Your kindness in every aspect of my life.*

*Please remove any lies or misconceptions that may undermine my belief in Your goodness and replace them with an assurance that You are good all the time. You don't change. Your Word says, "All things work together for good to those who love God," and I love You. In Jesus' name, Amen.*

# Day 15
# TRUTH #4: Believe God Loves You

*"We know, dear brothers and sisters, that God loves you and has chosen you to be His own people." 1 Thessalonians 1:4 (NLT)*

The fourth foundational truth to embrace is that not only does God exist, possess all power, and embody goodness, but He also loves you deeply and unconditionally. His love is a constant, choosing to be present in every moment of your life.

Despite this, Satan seeks to sow doubt about God's love for us because he understands how crucial this truth is to our faith.

How does the assurance of God's love impact your daily life and relationships?

_____

_____

Do you sometimes struggle to believe in God's love for you? Why or why not?

_____

_____

Here are three reasons Satan might want you to doubt God's love, along with Bible verses to counter these lies:

Satan wants you to doubt God's love to make you feel unworthy.

*"But God showed His great love for us by sending Christ to die for us while we were still sinners." Romans 5:8 (NLT)*

## Days 12 – 16  5 TRUTHS ABOUT GOD

How can reflecting on God's unconditional love for you, even when you feel unworthy, impact your sense of self-worth and relationship with Him?

_____

_____

_____

Satan wants you to question God's love during difficult times.

*"The Lord is good to all, and His tender mercies are over all His works."*
*Psalm 145:9*

How can recognizing that God's goodness and mercy extend through every trial help you trust in His love despite your current difficulties?

_____

_____

_____

Satan wants you to believe that God's love is temporary or conditional based on your behavior.

*"I have loved you, my people, with an everlasting love. With unfailing love I have drawn you to myself." Jeremiah 31:3 (NLT)*

How does understanding that God's love is everlasting and not dependent on your actions influence how you approach Him in both your successes and failures?

_____

_____

_____

As we explore the truth that God loves us unconditionally, it's vital to remember that His love is steadfast and unwavering. Despite any doubts, challenges, or feelings of unworthiness, God's love remains constant and eternal. Embracing this truth can transform our relationship with Him and deepen our faith, knowing that His love for us is perfect and never falters.

*Heavenly Father, thank You for Your unconditional love, which remains constant despite any doubts or lies that Satan may try to plant in my mind. Help me to see past the deceptions that question Your love and to fully grasp how deep, how wide, how high, and how long Your love is for me.*

*Strengthen my faith to overcome any fear or uncertainty and remind me of Your truth that Your love never falters and is always perfect. I love You because You first loved me. Let Your love flow through me and shine brightly in all I do today. In Jesus' name. Amen.*

# Day 16
# TRUTH #5: Believe God Keeps His Promises

*"And we know that God causes everything to work together for the good of those who love God and are called according to His purpose for them."*
Romans 8:28 (NLT)

The fifth essential truth to believe about God is that He promises to cause everything in your life to work together for good. This profound assurance is rooted in Romans 8:28, where we learn that God, in His infinite wisdom and love, weaves every circumstance, trial, and blessing into a tapestry that ultimately serves His great purpose for our lives. Even when things seem bleak or confusing, God's promise affirms that His plans for us are always for our benefit.

Satan aims to undermine our trust in God's promise of working all things for good because he knows that doubt in this area can erode our faith and hope. By making us question whether God truly has our best interests at heart, Satan seeks to instill unbelief, fear, discouragement, and frustration. He wants us to feel abandoned or to believe that our struggles are meaningless, which can lead us to lose hope and become disheartened in our walk with God.

How can recognizing that God is working all things together for your good reshape your perspective on the struggles you're facing and restore your hope?

What have you learned about God promising to work all things together for good?

_____

_____

_____

*"God has said, 'I will never fail you. I will never abandon you.'"*
*Hebrews 13:5 (NLT)*

How does understanding that God promises never to abandon you help you deal with feelings of abandonment or isolation during difficult times?

_____

_____

*"For our present troubles are small and won't last very long. Yet they produce for us a glory that vastly outweighs them and will last forever."*
*2 Corinthians 4:17 (NLT)*

How can focusing on the eternal glory that God promises help you see your current struggles in a new light and maintain hope despite temporary difficulties?

_____

_____

These verses and questions are designed to reaffirm God's constant presence and purpose in your life, countering feelings of abandonment and despair.

What have you learned about God promising to work all things together for good? Have you considered Romans 8:29?

_____

_____

## Days 12 – 16 5 TRUTHS ABOUT GOD

*"For God knew His people in advance, and He chose them to become like His Son, so that His Son would be the firstborn among many brothers and sisters." Romans 8:29 (NLT)*

In times of struggle and doubt, it's vital to remember that God's promises are steadfast and true. Even when we feel abandoned or question the meaning of our trials, we can trust that God is at work, turning every situation for our good and His glory. Romans 8:29 reminds us that God's ultimate purpose in working everything together for our good is to conform us to the image of His Son Jesus, making us more like Him and drawing us closer as His beloved children. It's no surprise that Satan doesn't want us to believe that God is a promise keeper. Embrace God's promises and allow them to renew your hope and strength in the journey.

*Heavenly Father, thank You for Your many promises that bring me peace, joy, hope, and assurance. I acknowledge that You are a promise keeper and that Your Word assures me that You work all things together for good. When I feel abandoned or struggle with doubts, remind me of Your faithfulness and the truth that Your purpose is to make me more like Jesus as Your son or daughter.*

*As I face difficulties, help me trust in Your goodness and embrace Your unconditional love. Strengthen my faith in Your promises each day and let me live with a deep conviction of Your existence and power. Help me to thank You in all things and to trust that You are guiding me toward Your good purposes. In Jesus' name, amen.*

# Days 17–21

# DEVOTIONAL PRAYERS

Throughout the Bible, we are instructed and encouraged to pray. Yet prayer doesn't mean that our struggles will go away or that our every request will be granted. Rather, when we pray, we are choosing to put our trust in God. Through our prayers, we turn over our concerns and allow Him to change the way we deal with our needs and desires.

God always hears our prayers and gives us peace to see us through each challenge. Sometimes, God may not answer our prayers the way we expect. However, we trust that He always has our best interests in mind. We trust that He knows best.

The truth is that intimacy develops as we seek God's face and sit in His presence, spending time in His Word and in prayer.

Many times, we think "prayer" means that we are running to God and asking Him to change our situations. But how often do we sit at His feet, praying, simply to get to know Him better? Or learn to trust Him more? In the end, those are the times that bear the greatest fruit and utterly transform us.

*The earnest prayer of a righteous person has great power and produces wonderful results. James 5:16 (NLT)*

The following devotionals are excerpts found in From My Heart to His: A Daily Devotional of Prayers, by Emily A. Edwards, Ph.D.

# Day 17
## Prayer for Evidence of the Fruit of the Spirit

Dear Lord,

You have given me the fruit of Your Spirit: love, joy, peace, patience, kindness, goodness, faithfulness, gentleness, and self-control. Thank You for each of these gifts. I pray that they would be evident in my life.

It is my choice to apply each fruit—a special gift with a special purpose—each day. Even on the days when I feel down or am struggling, I pray that I would choose the fruit of the Spirit over my fickle emotions. I pray that I would experience love, joy, and peace. Enable me to be patient, kind, good, faithful, and gentle. Help me to exercise self-control.

These qualities are important because when I walk in them, I am reflecting You. May others see that I belong to You and not to the world. Help me choose to show Your fruit rather than my connection to the world. The world cares little about the gifts of the Spirit but promotes everything that is in opposition to them. Thank You for first modeling these gifts so that we know how to walk in them too.

Your Spirit is so beautiful. I want to show the fruit of Your Spirit in all my relationships. At times, it seems so difficult, but You will help me. You love me so much, and You want me to be an encouragement. I know Your Spirit will be there with me and empower me, if I choose to listen.

In Your precious name I pray, amen.

> *But the Holy Spirit produces this kind of fruit in our lives: love, joy, peace, patience, kindness, goodness, faithfulness, gentleness, and self-control. There is no law against these things! Those who belong to Christ Jesus have nailed the passions and desires of their sinful nature to his cross and crucified them there. Since we are living by the Spirit, let us follow the Spirit's leading in every part of our lives.*
> *Galatians 5:22–25 (NLT)*

Days 17–21 DEVOTIONAL PRAYERS

Journal Your Thoughts

# Day 18
# Prayer for Guidance and Direction

Dear Jesus,

Life offers me many paths to take, and finding the right way can be confusing. I pray that I would always be able to look for and find You in every step I take. You have never led me astray, and I truly love to see the adventures on which You take me. Your path is straight. There are no deceiving curves or cliffs. The path is well lit and flat for safe walking. You being the guide helps me travel in peace through the chaos of the world. In all places, there are temptations of evil. Holy Spirit, I pray that You would steer me all clear of that.

I pray for those who are having a difficult time knowing which way to go in their lives. I pray that they would look to You and search Your Word for direction. I pray they would not seek the world's opinion, for in doing so, they will be surely led astray.

I pray that You would send someone to help point them Your way. The words of a true friend can act as a calming balm on their minds and hearts. Encouragement from fellow brothers and sisters is needed for everyone. Doing this consciously helps in the growing of their faith. It is all orchestrated by You, Jesus.

I pray this in Your precious name, amen.

*The Lord says, "I will guide you along the best pathway for your life. I will advise you and watch over you." Psalm 32:8 (NLT)*

Days 17–21 DEVOTIONAL PRAYERS

## Journal Your Thoughts

# Day 19
# Prayer for a Renewed Mind

Dear Heavenly Father,

Sometimes things need to die before new life can appear. A seed must die before it can start to grow. My wrong thinking and focusing on things that are not of You need to die. They must die to make room for the more valuable thoughts and experiences that You want to give me. What You have is better than what the world offers.

Lord, I pray that I would make the choice every day to renew my mind. I want to flush out the bad and pour in Your good. In a state of renewal, I feel recreated. But I cannot do this on my own. It is only through Your hand. For renewal to occur, my mind must be focused on You and Your goodness and not on things of this world.

There is so much pain around me. Instead of dwelling on that pain, help me to see it through Your eyes. Rather than becoming bitter and pointing fingers, You invite me to join You in what You are doing. I must listen carefully and obey. If I resist, I will lose the blessing of seeing what You can do through me.

Often, I feel inadequate. The tasks that You set before me seem too big for me to handle. The truth is that they are too big for me to handle, but You are not asking me to take on these challenges alone. You are asking me to take on these challenges with You by my side. You will strengthen and empower me to do what You have called me to do.

In the name of Jesus I pray, amen.

*Don't copy the behavior and customs of this world, but let God transform you into a new person by changing the way you think. Then you will learn to know God's will for you, which is good and pleasing and perfect.*
*Romans 12:2 (NLT)*

Days 17–21 DEVOTIONAL PRAYERS

## Journal Your Thoughts

# Day 20
# Prayer Against Double-Mindedness

Dear Abba, Father,

Depending on what is happening at any given moment, my attitude can change like the wind. I pray that I would not rely on my circumstances to dictate my choices. I want my love for You, not the world, to drive my every decision.

I pray for those who continually struggle with double-mindedness. I am thinking of the ones who have so much to offer, but their decision-making flip-flops depending on their circumstances. I pray that they would draw closer to You so that You can strengthen them from the inside out. No more do they need to be slaves to the things happening around them, but a free person in Christ.

That is exciting to know that I can choose to be consistent in my choices. The world does not decide whether my choices are consistent or not—I do. If I relied on the wisdom of the world, I would fail most of the time. If I choose to be full of the joy and wisdom of Christ, I will live an abundant life. Your power, Lord, will surge through me, and I will not fear but trust in You. Thank You!

In Jesus' name I pray, amen.

*Do not waver, for a person with divided loyalty is as unsettled as a wave of the sea that is blown and tossed by the wind. Such people should not expect to receive anything from the Lord. Their loyalty is divided between God and the world, and they are unstable in everything they do. James 1:6–8 (NLT)*

Days 17–21 DEVOTIONAL PRAYERS

## Journal Your Thoughts

# Day 21
## The Benefits of Choosing God's Way

*Trust in the LORD with all your heart, and lean not on your own understanding; in all your ways acknowledge Him, and He shall direct your paths. Proverbs 3:5–6*

Have you ever wondered what it means to go God's way? It's not just about receiving Jesus as our Savior and securing our place in heaven, but it's also about choosing to follow God daily and allowing His Spirit to lead us. When we make this decision, incredible benefits await us. Let's explore some of them:

1. **Eternal Life:** By accepting Jesus as our Savior, we gain the gift of eternal life with God. This means that no matter what challenges we face in this world, we have the assurance of spending eternity in perfect fellowship with Him.

2. **Forgiveness and Redemption:** Through Jesus, we receive forgiveness for our sins and are redeemed from the eternal consequences of our mistakes. We no longer need to carry the weight of guilt, shame, and regret. Instead, we can embrace the freedom found in God's loving grace.

3. **Inner Peace and Joy:** Following God's Spirit brings a profound sense of peace and joy into our lives. Even in the midst of difficult circumstances, we can experience a peace that surpasses all understanding, knowing that God is with us and that He is in control.

4. **Guidance and Direction:** God's Spirit serves as our faithful guide, providing wisdom and direction for our daily decisions. When we submit our ways to Him, He illuminates the path we should walk, helping us to make choices aligned with His will.

5. **Strength and Power:** As we go God's way, we tap into His infinite strength and power. He equips us to face challenges, overcome obstacles, and live out the purpose He has designed for us. We no longer need to rely solely on our own abilities but can trust in His unfailing provision.

Days 17–21 DEVOTIONAL PRAYERS

Application Questions:

1. Reflect on your own journey of following God. How have you experienced the benefits mentioned above? Take a moment to thank God for His goodness and faithfulness in your life.

_____

_____

_____

2. Are there areas in your life where you find it challenging to go God's way? Identify them and bring them before God in prayer. Ask for His strength and guidance to align those areas with His will.

_____

_____

_____

3. How can you intentionally lean on God's understanding instead of your own? Consider how you can cultivate a deeper dependence on His wisdom and seek His guidance in all aspects of your life.

_____

_____

_____

4. Is there anyone in your life who needs to experience the benefits of going God's way? Pray for opportunities to share the love of Christ with them and be a witness of the transformation God has brought into your own life.

_____

_____

Remember, choosing to go God's way is not just a one-time decision but a daily surrender of our lives to His loving guidance. As we follow His Spirit, we will continue to experience the abundant blessings and benefits He has prepared for us.

Prayer: Heavenly Father, thank You for the incredible benefits we receive when we choose to follow You. Help us to trust in Your wisdom, submit our ways to You, and experience the fullness of life found in going Your way. Strengthen us to live as faithful witnesses of Your love and grace. In Jesus' name, amen.

You have completed our 21-Day Challenge for Change. Let's pray.

*Heavenly Father, as I conclude this 21-Day Challenge for Change, I come before You with a heart full of gratitude and reflection. Over the past days, I have journeyed through understanding how to make decisions guided by Your wisdom, explored the Belief Tree to uncover and address the lies I have believed, and delved into the five foundational truths about who You are.*

*I am grateful for the opportunity to confront and replace false beliefs with Your unchanging truth. The truth of Your character—Your goodness, Your care for me, Your desire for a close relationship, and Your unconditional love—has become a solid foundation upon which I can build.*

*The five devotional prayers have been a source of strength and guidance, reminding me of Your promises and faithfulness. I ask that You continue to deepen my understanding and application of these truths in my life.*

*Help me to carry forward the lessons I've learned, holding fast to Your truth and letting it shape every aspect of my life. May Your wisdom guide my decisions, and may Your love and grace be reflected in all I say and do. In Jesus' name, I pray, Amen.*

# GRACE YOUR TABLE

## *SUGAR-FREE DESSERT RECIPES FOR YOU & GRACE'S MOM*

### SUGAR-FREE CHEESECAKE CUPCAKES

*Crust:*
½ cup almond flour
¼ cup granulated, no-calorie brown sugar sweetener
½ cup of butter, melted

*Filling:*
2 (8 ounce) packages cream cheese, softened at room temperature
2 large eggs
¾ cup of granulated, no-calorie sweetener (such as erythritol, allulose, or stevia)
1 tsp of vanilla extract

*Serve with:*
1 cup of heavy whipping cream
Mixed berries

1. Preheat your oven to 350°F (175°C). Line 12 muffin cups with paper liners.

2. In a mixing bowl, combine the almond flour and brown sugar sweetener. Mix in the melted butter until well combined.

3. Spoon mixture into the bottoms of the paper lined cups and press into a flat crust.

4. Bake for 10–12 minutes, until lightly golden. Set aside to cool.

5. In a mixing bowl, beat the cream cheese, eggs, sweetener, and vanilla until smooth.

6. Pour the cheesecake batter over the crust layer in the paper-lined cups and smooth the top with a spatula.

7. Bake for 15–20 minutes until the cheesecake is set but still slightly jiggly in the center.

8. Let the cheesecakes cool and then refrigerate for several hours.

9. Serve chilled with whipped cream and berries.

*Coffee + Cheesecake = Enjoy :)*

## HEALTHY PEANUT BUTTER CUPS

*Crust:*
¾ cup peanut butter
½ cup almond flour
¼ cup granulated, no-calorie brown sugar sweetener
Dash of salt

*Filling:*
9-ounce package sugar-free chocolate chips (stevia-sweetened)
2 large eggs
1 tsp of coconut oil

1. Mix the peanut butter, almond flour, eggs, and coconut oil together until smooth and dry enough to make little balls.

2. Add sweetener with a dash of salt and mix. Set aside.

3. Melt the chocolate chips for 30 seconds in the microwave. Stir and add another 30 seconds until silky smooth.

4. Line the muffin tin with paper cups or use a silicone cupcake pan on a cookie sheet.

5. Fill each cup less than halfway with chocolate using a small spoon.

6. Make a ball of peanut butter mixture and drop into each cup.

7. Pour chocolate on top of each to cover.

8. Refrigerate for 20 minutes or until hardened.

9. Enjoy!

GRACE YOUR TABLE

# ABOUT THE AUTHORS

DR. EMILY A. EDWARDS is a captivating speaker, gifted writer, and compassionate counselor. She frequently travels across the United States and abroad, leading impactful seminars and retreats. Emily holds a Master's in Biblical Counseling from Victorious Christian Life Institute and earned her PhD in Christian Counseling from Vision International University. She is a Licensed Clinical Pastoral Counselor, passionate about bringing God's healing and wholeness to those who have experienced pain and rejection in any area of their lives.

Emily and her close friend, co-author Valerie, have been collaborating for many years, sharing a deep love for teaching biblical principles regarding relationships, identity in Christ, and forgiveness. Valerie affectionately describes Emily as "half counselor, half author, and the other half comedian."

Emily and Michael Medanich were married in 2022.

DR. VALERIE NYSTROM PAINE is a published author and inspiring speaker. In 1999, she and her husband, Fred, joined the staff of Victorious Christian Living International in Goodyear, Arizona. They touch many lives through their counseling, dynamic teaching, engaging webinars, and transformative Bible studies.

As the Director of Material Development and Media, Valerie played a crucial role in the creation of the Seven Areas of Life Training® (SALT), Kids SALT, and e-Bible 101 programs. She has also collaborated with Emily on two other books: *Grace Letters and Table Grace*.

Valerie holds a Bachelor of Education degree from Washburn University in Topeka, Kansas. She earned her Master's in Biblical Leadership and Doctorate in Biblical Counseling from Victorious Christian Life Institute.

Married since 1987, Fred and Valerie are grateful for their wonderful family.

Made in the USA
Columbia, SC
20 April 2025